Seemed Like Nothing Could Distract Him From Thoughts Of The Nightmare That Had Awakened Him.

Harlan stared up at the full moon from the deck of his sailboat. Just then, a movement on the dock drew his gaze. It was a woman, unmistakably, her body curved and graceful, her hair gleaming in the silver light.

Emma.

Well, maybe *one* thing could distract him, he thought.

What *was* it about her? They had nothing in common—and she'd all but accused him of being involved in the mystery that had brought her here. And yet he couldn't stop thinking about her.

He stayed where he was and watched as she stepped onto the deck of her boat and disappeared below, never having even glanced his way.

With a sigh, he gave up on any idea of more sleep tonight….

Dear Reader,

Welcome to another compelling month of powerful, passionate and provocative love stories from Silhouette Desire. You asked for it…you got it…more Dynasties! Our newest continuity, DYNASTIES: THE DANFORTHS, launches this month with Barbara McCauley's *The Cinderella Scandal.* Set in Savannah, Georgia, and filled with plenty of family drama and sensuality, this new twelve-book series will thrill you for the entire year.

There is one sexy air force pilot to be found between the pages of the incomparable Merline Lovelace's *Full Throttle,* part of her TO PROTECT AND DEFEND series. And the fabulous Justine Davis is back in Silhouette Desire with *Midnight Seduction,* a fiery tale in her REDSTONE, INCORPORATED series.

If it's a whirlwind Vegas wedding you're looking for (and who isn't?) then be sure to pick up the third title in Katherine Garbera's KING OF HEARTS miniseries, *Let It Ride.* The fabulous TEXAS CATTLEMAN'S CLUB: THE STOLEN BABY series continues this month with Kathie DeNosky's tale of unforgettable passion, *Remembering One Wild Night.* And finally, welcome new author Amy Jo Cousins to the Desire lineup with her superhot contribution, *At Your Service.*

I hope all of the Silhouette Desire titles this month will fulfill your every fantasy.

Melissa Jeglinski

Melissa Jeglinski
Senior Editor, Silhouette Desire

Please address questions and book requests to:
Silhouette Reader Service
U.S.: 3010 Walden Ave., P.O. Box 1325, Buffalo, NY 14269
Canadian: P.O. Box 609, Fort Erie, Ont. L2A 5X3

Midnight Seduction

JUSTINE DAVIS

Silhouette® Desire

Published by Silhouette Books

America's Publisher of Contemporary Romance

SILHOUETTE BOOKS

ISBN 0-373-76557-6

MIDNIGHT SEDUCTION

JUSTINE DAVIS

lives in Kingston, Washington. Her interests outside of writing are sailing, doing needlework, horseback riding and driving her restored 1967 Corvette roadster—top down, of course.

A former policewoman, Justine says that years ago, a young man she worked with encouraged her to try for a promotion to a position that was, at that time, occupied only by men. "I succeeded, became wrapped up in my new job and that man moved away, never, I thought, to be heard from again. Ten years later he appeared out of the woods of Washington State, saying he'd never forgotten me and would I please marry him. With that history, how could I write anything but romance?"

One

The tide had to turn soon. Didn't it?

Emma Purcell tried to tune out the noise of the jet's engines and concentrate. Her business was barely staying above water anyway, and at this rate, with Frank Kean's demands for higher rent, Safe Haven was going to go under soon. Unless she found a sizable life preserver, they would—

Emma cut off her thoughts and smothered a sigh. Ever since she'd left the attorney's office, she—who didn't even like the sea—had been thinking in watery metaphors. She'd wanted a distraction from the aching grief of her cousin Wayne's untimely death and the financial woes of her beloved animal shelter, Safe Haven, and now she had one. A big one. And it was all wrapped up in one huge question.

Why on earth had Wayne left his ocean-hating cousin a boat?

Maybe I can sell it, she thought as the pilot announced the presence of the remains of Mt. St. Helens on the right side of the airplane. *Might get enough to keep us going for a couple of months. Maybe even more, with luck. Hey, maybe I could even get a haircut!*

But she would fulfill Wayne's request first, she told herself. As he'd asked of her in the cryptic letter she'd received—eerily—three days after he'd died, she would look at the *Pretty Lady* in person before she did anything. She owed him that much at least.

Emma fought the wave of sadness threatening to swamp her again. She made herself look out the window as they neared SeaTac airport. It looked beautiful here in the Pacific Northwest, she admitted. She'd never been to this part of the country before, and now she wondered why. It was true she wasn't fond of the ocean, but this was different. From the air Puget Sound seemed more like a huge, calm lake, dotted with islands and edged with peninsulas large and small.

The ocean had always seemed so vast and frightening to her, and had since her childhood. Silly, of course, but there it was. But this felt safer somehow. It wasn't just the lack of crashing waves, it was that you were never out of sight of land here, and that was comforting to her landlubber's soul.

"This won't be so bad," she told herself as she signed the papers for her small rental car. "Maybe this can really turn out to be like a vacation after all."

And then the smiling young man behind the counter blithely told her it was a breeze to get to her destination from here, she simply headed up I-5, got off at exit 177 and headed for the ferry that would deposit her on the other side within a few miles of the very marina she wanted.

Ferry? Other side?

Images of Charon and his dark boat gliding across the River Styx flitted through her suddenly panicked mind. She shoved aside the image and studied the map on which the young man was drawing her route.

Once she was outside the terminal, she pulled out her cell phone to place the promised call to Sheila, her indefatigable assistant at Safe Haven.

"I'm here, safe and sound," she said. "How are things there?"

"Fine. I stalled off the county, and Mrs. Santini's son came and picked up Corky."

"She's going home?"

Emma could almost hear Sheila smiling. "Yes, tomorrow. He wanted Corky there to greet her."

Warmth flooded Emma at the thought of the reunion between the sweet, gentle elderly woman and her beloved terrier. This was what made all the work, the long hours, the strain of approaching strangers and begging for money or supplies, worth it. This was what Safe Haven was for, to take care of pets when their sick or injured owners couldn't.

"I'll check back with you tonight," she said.

"Don't you dare," Sheila said sternly. "You're on your first vacation in two years."

"But—"

"You trying to insult me, girlfriend? Saying I can't run this place without you?"

Sheila's anger was feigned, but Emma knew the sentiment was not. She also knew Sheila could handle things quite competently, that it was only her ambivalence making her nervous. She let the woman reassure her, and disconnected with a promise not to call again unless it was an emergency.

As Emma drove she tried to distract herself. She made herself focus on her surroundings, thinking she owed it to Wayne to at least open herself to whatever he'd found here that had made him stay so far from home.

Not that Wayne had anything to come home for, she thought, her mouth twisting. It was hard not to be more bitter than ever now. His family's cruelty had driven Wayne away long ago, and now he was dead with that rift never mended. Not for lack of trying on her part; she'd tried countless times to be the go-between, to help Wayne establish some kind of relationship with his family. But she'd failed. Even her parents hadn't been much help.

It didn't matter anymore, she told herself before the old anger could build. Wayne was dead, so he could no longer be an embarrassment to his stuffy, self-righteous parents.

Emma bit her lip to stop the tears that threatened to flow yet again, and tried to stop thinking about it. When that minor pain didn't work, she thought about the fact that she would soon be driving this little roller skate of a car onto a boat that was going to head out to sea. Well, not exactly out to sea, but still…

That seemed to work, and kept her occupied until she had to steel herself to actually drive onto the huge green and white Washington state ferry. It was so big it seemed silly to be afraid, especially when she saw how casually the other passengers took it all, chattering happily as they headed upstairs for a snack or a drink.

"The drink part I understand," Emma muttered to herself, thinking uncharacteristically of something alcoholic. And the last thing she needed was a snack, not when she was trying to get rid of those extra twenty pounds she'd somehow picked up.

But by the time the boat actually left the dock she had a muffin in her hand, and she was surprised to note she actually felt like eating it. And had no desire to dull her senses with anything liquid.

Maybe this boat thing wouldn't be so bad after all.

They'd told him it would take time. What they hadn't told him was how much.

Harlan McClaren rubbed at the polished chrome cleat on the *Seahawk*'s rail, although it had been gleaming spotlessly for some time now. He rubbed at it with full concentration, as if it were a complex task instead of mindless routine. He rubbed at it as if his life depended on it. He knew his sanity did.

He also knew it was going to exhaust him. That was what boggled him more than anything else, how utterly exhausted the simplest of tasks left him. He'd just turned thirty-nine but imagined this was what seventy must feel like. It was as if he was constantly moving underwater, as if the air itself had taken to resisting his every move.

Yet he welcomed the exhaustion. It kept him from thinking too much, and if he could make sure he was tired enough, he sometimes slept without dreaming. Or without dreams he remembered, anyway.

His shoulder was starting to ache, a souvenir of the mess that had landed him here. He flexed then stretched it instead of stopping the work that aggravated it and going for ice and a compression wrap, as the therapists had told him he should. Which, Harlan thought wryly, would surprise no one who knew him. Especially Josh, owner of the *Seahawk,* who had sent Harlan to recuperate on the boat with stern instructions to behave during his forced recuperation.

"For once in your life, Mac, do the safe thing," had been his actual words. Joshua Redstone knew him as well as anyone.

He heard the creak of the gangway as somebody headed down to the dock. He thought about dodging inside the cabin, not feeling up to casual conversation with any of the marina regulars today. But after a moment the quality of the steps, the hesitancy in them, reached him. He looked up. And frowned.

The woman coming down the slanted wood walkway was holding on to the pipe railing as if her life depended on it. She hadn't, as some he'd seen this summer, worn ridiculously high-heeled or platform sandals to visit a marina, but she was walking as if she had done just that. Tiny steps, as if she expected the boards beneath her feet to collapse and spill her into the chilly sound at any moment.

He turned back to his polishing once she was down on the dock itself, expecting her to stop at one of the boat slips long before she reached the large one near the end that berthed the *Seahawk*. Instead the footsteps continued, coming closer and closer, until his movements stopped and he crouched frozen beside the well-polished cleat. He could see a distorted, fun house mirror sort of reflection in the shiny surface, only enough to see that she had short, sandy-blond hair.

He held his breath. He was expecting no one, was here to avoid dealing with people just now. He'd had no visitors since he'd been here, and he liked it that way.

Puzzlement overcame him when the woman continued down the dock past the two empty slips between the *Seahawk* and the next boat. The boat that was at the visitor's berth, the side tie at the end of the dock. The worse for weather *Pretty Lady*.

The boat that belonged to a dead man.

Harlan sat back on his heels, watching now. If he'd thought she hadn't noticed him, the quick, darting glance she gave him over her shoulder disproved the idea. And the sudden quickening of her pace told him what this particular woman thought of his looks just now.

He frowned at his own thought. Any woman headed for the *Pretty Lady* was hardly the type to be picky. But then, she didn't look like the sort that he'd seen on the few occasions when there'd been a female visitor to that particular vessel. Too classy, too pulled together for that kind.

Maybe she was some attorney, come to assess the value of the thing. Which was lessening by the day, he thought. Then he turned away rather forcefully.

It's none of your business, he told himself, and went back to polishing the cleat that didn't need it. He didn't care, and didn't want to care why someone had finally shown up at the old scow.

And then the image of the woman played back in his head, his weary brain summoned up another image, and he made the connection he should have made the moment he saw her. The resemblance to the man from the *Pretty Lady* was unmistakable. This had to be the cousin Wayne Purcell had spoken of. The only family member he'd ever spoken of with affection rather than anger or downright hatred.

The thought flitted into his mind that he should go express his condolences. He hadn't been close to Wayne, but they had shared a beer on occasion—that is until he'd realized that once Wayne started drinking the man had a problem stopping. But Harlan couldn't bestir himself to move. The thought of approaching a stranger, a woman, an attractive one at that, and being kind and sympathetic seemed as impossible as climbing Everest.

He watched her out of the corner of his eye as she picked her way with great care up the steps beside the sailboat, grasping the railing as she had above, with a sort of desperate care. When she finally got on board, she moved gingerly to the main cabin and stood looking blankly at the hatchway. She obviously knew little about boats. In fact, if he had to guess, he'd say she was afraid of them.

Not your problem, he told himself. And turned to his work once more. Soon the metal was growing warm from his efforts. And he kept at it, repeating to himself that it was none of his business. He finally convinced himself. Until he heard the loud thump.

And the scream.

It was a miracle she hadn't broken a leg, or worse, Emma thought. Not that that did anything for the ache in her hip or the horrible burst of pain that had erupted from her elbow and dizzied her. She sat up gingerly, cradling the arm that had made her cry out in shock and pain.

Her breathing had just begun to slow down when a sound from above made it quicken again. The slight dip of the boat told her what it was; someone had boarded behind her. Before she could scramble to her feet the light coming in the hatchway vanished as a man blocked the opening.

Calm down, she told herself. *You're not in the big city now, there's no reason to panic.*

And then the man spoke, and confirmed her thoughts; he didn't sound at all threatening.

"Are you all right?"

In fact, she thought, he sounded tired. Very tired. As if he very much didn't want to be there.

Well, of course, she thought. *He was probably an experienced nautical type, reluctant to come to the rescue of yet another newbie.*

When she didn't immediately answer he came down a few steps into the cabin, and she realized he was the man she'd seen before, on the big, sleek, expensive-looking powerboat in the last occupied slip.

The man whose appearance had made her hasten past him. And here he was, at a moment when she felt more stupid than she had in recent memory.

He came down the rest of the steps in a rush, and she realized she'd waited too long to answer.

"No, I'm all right," she said, throwing up a hand as if that would ward him off. Then she got a clearer look at him in the light that streamed through the portholes, and she thought she might be able to do just that. He was almost painfully thin, and the deck shoes, jeans and Henley style shirt he wore were very new, as if the thinness was also recent and he'd had to buy new clothes to fit. His thick, tousled brown hair had the golden streaks of someone who spent time in the sun, but he was pale. And his eyes had the hollow look of someone who'd been ill. Or still was.

Or maybe someone who indulged in substances that killed the appetite and revved the motor until this gaunt look was the result, she thought suspiciously. She had no firsthand experience with anyone like that, but you

didn't live in Southern California for long without seeing it. He had that wary, edgy look as well, making
eyes that were a striking shade of green alarming rather
than attractive. Or so she told herself.

"You're sure?" he asked, and she got the oddest
feeling he was desperately hoping she would say yes.
So he wouldn't have to do anything, get involved, call
for help? she wondered.

"I'm fine," she told him firmly. "I misjudged the
steepness of the steps, that's all."

The sensible words seemed to reassure him. He
shifted his weight and leaned back until he was sitting
on one of the steps that had tripped her up. She wondered if he planned on staying a while, or if she'd been
right in thinking he was simply tired.

"Never been on a sailboat before?"

She flushed. But he wasn't looking at her with
amusement, only a mild interest, so she admitted the
truth. "Any boat," she said.

He studied her for a long moment. She got slowly to
her feet, grateful that everything seemed to be in working order; she hadn't been certain that she hadn't done
some real damage. Then he spoke again, stunning her
into stillness.

"You're Emma, aren't you?"

She nearly gasped. How on earth…? "How did you
know that?"

He shrugged. "It was no great leap. Wayne talked
about you. And you look like him. Same eyes, and
nose."

She flushed again. Her eyes were like Wayne's, nice
enough, a medium blue she liked because she could
make them appear gray or deep blue or even teal depending on what color she wore. But her nose was the

bane of her existence and always had been. The upward tilt at the end had doomed her to a life of being called perky, cute, impish and any number of other inane descriptors she had come to hate. Wayne had indeed had that same feature, and had hated it for the same reasons. It was worse for him, he'd always insisted. On a girl it *was* perky, cute and impish, but on a guy it was cause for endless teasing.

Belatedly she realized the implications of what this man had said. "You knew Wayne?"

He nodded. "Casually. It was hard not to, when he was docked so close and I'm here all the time."

Realization struck. Her gaze flicked to the tote bag that had slid across the heavily marked teak floor when she'd taken her fall, as if she could read Wayne's letter through the canvas. Not that she needed to. Eerie as its arrival had been, she remembered it perfectly.

If you need anything, ask McClaren, he'd written. *He's a local marina bum living on some rich guy's yacht, but I think you can trust him.*

Well, the boat she'd seen him on certainly qualified as "some rich guy's yacht." And his appearance matched what she'd expect from a marina bum. She wondered what rich guy would trust this ominous-looking man with his boat.

But he had been working when she'd gone past. So at least he was doing something in return for the charity. But she still didn't trust his looks, and resolved both to get him out of here now, and to avoid him as much as possible from now on. That there might be more to it than wariness, she refused to admit.

"No one else came with you? He mentioned his parents were still alive."

His expression was faintly puzzled, not a frown but

more a vaguely quizzical look, as if a frown would require too much effort. She wondered why he'd even asked if he was so bored. Or so tired, she amended; the dark circles under his eyes seemed to point toward the accuracy of that impression.

She hesitated in responding to his comment, then decided it hardly mattered to this stranger. And at this point she felt little loyalty to her beloved cousin's judgmental parents anyway.

"He was dead to them," she said, "and had been for some time."

He seemed to take a moment to absorb that. "That explains a lot," he finally said.

Emma didn't miss the implications this time. She did a quick reassessment. If this man had known Wayne well enough to say that, he could be the best source of information, and she didn't want to antagonize him.

"What did Wayne do while he was here? I didn't even know he was up here."

She knew she wasn't imagining his withdrawal. His face, which had shown only the slightest interest, went utterly blank. The only thing left was a weariness that made even his strong features seem to slump slightly.

"I don't know," he said, and she had the oddest feeling he was lying. About what, she didn't know, nor could she say why she felt that way.

He began to turn, as if to head back up the steps and out of the boat's cabin.

"When did you last see him?" she asked, desperate for any connection from someone who had had contact with Wayne recently.

He paused, his head still turned away from her. She

thought she saw a shiver go through him, although she couldn't imagine why. Finally, slowly and with obvious reluctance, he answered her.

"An hour before he died."

Two

Harlan knew he'd left her there gaping at him as he escaped, knew he'd opened himself up to more questions than he ever wanted to answer. He wasn't sure what had made him say what he had, only that the note of desperate need in her voice had gotten to him. His armor against that kind of thing wasn't as solid as it used to be. Perhaps because he'd been reduced to desperation himself not so long ago. Certainly not because she was looking at him with those huge blue eyes.

The old nightmare images threatened to rise again, the damp, cold cellar, the ropes digging into his flesh, the agony of being unable to move more than a few inches, the horror of the footsteps on the stairs that heralded another beating or burning, another agonizing session of demands that he confess to things he knew nothing about.

He fought them down, focusing instead on the pretty woman on the inaccurately named *Pretty Lady.*

He was glad she hadn't been able to react quickly enough to stop him from getting out of there. And he couldn't deny he was headed back to the *Seahawk* at a fast clip, hoping to get out of sight before she collected herself enough to come after him. Once inside, he could ignore her if she did show up. He nearly groaned aloud at the image of himself, hiding, while the woman who had grabbed his attention at first sight pounded on his door.

He finally accomplished his goal, locking the main salon door behind him and quickly darting out of sight down the steps to the safety of his lower stateroom. He sank down on his bunk, only now aware of how quickly he was breathing, and how his heart was racing. He was just short of shaking, and the realization was almost unbearably glum.

Harlan leaned forward, burying his face in his hands. He'd thought he was making progress, thought he'd come a long way since his nightmare had finally ended. He'd even thought he might be ready to leave here soon. But if a five minute conversation with a stranger had this effect on him, he still had a long, long way to go.

But he'd had to run. He could feel her need to talk, to know about the last days of her cousin's life. She'd had many more questions, he could sense them waiting to be fired at him. So he'd done the only thing he could do. He'd removed the target.

Steadier now, he got to his feet. He left the small stateroom—Josh had told him to use the master stateroom, but he'd never been able to bring himself to do so—and walked to the workroom where he'd set up his computer. His personal affairs had suffered from his long absence, and he thought perhaps some time spent wrestling with those problems might calm him. At least they would take some concentration.

If he was lucky, the maneuverings and stratagems would lure him in and he could lose a few hours in the pursuits that had fascinated him ever since he'd had enough money to play the game. And the game was much more cutthroat and dangerous than it had been when he'd started.

He knew the consensus of the marina population, if they thought of him at all, was that he was a bum taking advantage of his rich friend, his computer setup something to play games on or worse. He was simply too weary to try and change the impression. He was too weary even to care what anyone thought of him.

Funny how he'd forgotten that weariness for a few moments in his rush to escape Emma Purcell.

Emma supposed she'd been more embarrassed in her life, but she couldn't remember when. Nor had she ever sent a man—to her knowledge, anyway—running so quickly.

She'd not had much luck with men, it was true. She acknowledged that to herself as, sure now she wasn't injured beyond some certain-to-develop bruises and a scrape on her left forearm, she checked her clothes for any damage from her fall. But she knew her lack of luck was because of her poor judgment rather than her looks. While she wasn't beautiful, she wasn't repellent, either.

Not that you could prove it by the man from the big boat, she thought. He'd been clearly reluctant to be here in the first place, and once he was sure she was all right, it seemed he couldn't wait to get away. Not that she'd wanted him to stick around. He still scared her more than a little, with that "on the edge of wild" look in his eyes. And the fact that she kept thinking about him didn't make her happier.

But he had come to her aid, Emma reminded herself. He'd been kind enough to be worried, and he'd talked enough about other things to get her past her initial chagrin.

Other things. Wayne.

She'd been avoiding thinking about his shocking last words. She'd focused on her embarrassment at her ungainly tumble so she couldn't think about them. But now she sat down on the threadbare cushion of the banquette that apparently served the sailboat as a dining area. The table itself was scarred and dented, but looked fairly clean. She leaned forward to rest on it, then cradled her head in her hands.

Wayne talked about you...

The ache those words caused in a heart not yet resigned to the permanency of this loss was almost more than she could bear. Especially knowing what the police had said, that Wayne had died cold and alone, drowning in these dark waters that made her so edgy.

And that McClaren man had been with him that night. Or at least had seen Wayne, still alive. Maybe he was the last one who had.

Her mind recoiled again, and she distracted herself with the realization that she wasn't really sure that the man was the McClaren Wayne had mentioned, although the marina bum description certainly fit. He hadn't offered his name, and hadn't had to ask for hers, so she hadn't even thought to confirm her guess. But she was certain she was right. It all fit too neatly.

An hour before he died, he'd said.

And the police had said Wayne was drunk. Very drunk, with a blood-alcohol level disturbingly high. She couldn't imagine Wayne that way. Sure, he'd toyed with alcohol and cigarettes when they were kids, but he'd never been out of control. And when they'd been older, and she'd been devastated after finding her supposed fiancé intimately entwined with a beautiful coworker, he'd lectured her that she wouldn't find peace at the bottom of a bottle. It hadn't even occurred to her to seek relief in booze, if for no other reason than she hated the taste of the stuff, but she'd thought his concern touching, and loved him all the more for it.

Had Wayne forgotten his own advice and been looking for some kind of peace in that bottle? Had the ostracism of his family finally collected its toll? Had he—

She cut off her musings as another thought struck her. Had they been drinking together, Wayne and McClaren? Was that why he'd been so drunk? She could imagine that, Wayne drinking too much with someone else who did. Just like the time he'd gone along with an older boy's joyride in a "borrowed" car, or let some of the wilder kids lead him into trouble he never would have gotten into on his own; sometimes Wayne just didn't say no when he should.

So had McClaren contributed to her cousin's death? Had he encouraged him to drink more than he could handle, then let him wander off in this warren of docks and narrow gangways even knowing he was so intoxicated?

She sighed, knowing that if she wanted answers to those questions she was going to have to deal with that man again. Probably again and again, she amended silently, because it wasn't something he would likely admit to easily.

"You can't do anything about that right now," she told herself aloud. *And,* she added silently, *you'd better get started here. Look around and see what you're dealing with.*

Instead, she found herself digging into her tote bag, searching the now tossed contents for the envelope that held Wayne's letter. It had arrived the worse for wear, looking as if he'd reused an old envelope by crossing out the original name and address. As she pulled it out now, she realized something she hadn't before; that envelope had been addressed to Harlan McClaren. There was what appeared to be a business logo of some kind printed where the return address would go, but Wayne had also crossed that out so well she couldn't tell what it had been.

She pulled out the note he'd written. When she'd first received the letter she'd let it sit unopened for a couple of days. After the news of his death, she'd been shattered anew by this message when she knew Wayne had died the day after he'd mailed it. Especially since she hadn't heard from him in so long. To have it happen now, like this...

When she finally had opened it, she'd been more puzzled than ever. It had been full of apologies and rambling explanations, but had ended with a rather ominous statement that no matter what happened, she should "look to the *Pretty Lady* for the answer. She holds her secrets deep, but they're there."

And now he was dead. Her charming, excitable, impulsive cousin. Those flashing blue eyes closed forever, the silver tongue that got him into trouble as often as out, permanently stilled. She wondered if his parents— or her own for that matter—regretted their harsh treatment of him now.

On the thought her cell phone rang. It was a very comforting sound, because she had wondered if she'd even be able to get a signal out here. She dug into her purse and pulled out the phone.

The comfort level inspired by successful communication dropped the moment she saw the call was from her parents. They had been gone when she'd made the decision to fly up here, so she'd only left them a message on their answering machine, secretly glad she didn't have to talk to them in person. They would have tried to talk her out of it, as they had always tried to talk her out of anything to do with Wayne.

She thought about letting the call go to her voice mail, but while she knew the conversation would be unpleasant, she also knew it would have to be faced eventually.

"Might as well be now," she muttered as she pushed the button and put the phone to her ear.

"Emma? What are you doing? You can't be serious about this, running off to the middle of nowhere!"

Her mother's voice had that slightly elevated pitch that told Emma the woman would be wringing her hands if she wasn't holding the receiver. She probably did have her other hand pressed against her chest, as if her wayward daughter were about to give her a heart attack. Margaret Purcell always did have a dramatic streak in her.

"Actually, Mom, it's quite beautiful," she said, keeping her voice casual and her tone upbeat.

"You mean you're already there?"

Her father's voice this time, booming out over the line as usual; he'd obviously picked up an extension.

"Yes, Dad. I'm already here. And," she added, determined to nip this early, "I'm glad I came. This is a lovely place."

"With all that water?" her mother asked. "You hate water. You have ever since you fell off that boat when you were a child."

"I hate the ocean," she pointed out. "This is different."

"Never mind that," her father put in brusquely, as he always did whenever he thought the women in his life were wandering too far from what he'd decided was the subject at hand. "I want to know what you're doing there at all. Surely there are people there who could handle the selling of that boat for you."

"I'm sure there are," she agreed. "But I wanted to see it, first."

"Because it was Wayne's?" her mother guessed.

"Nothing that boy could leave you could be worth much," her father said gruffly. "He ended just like we said he would, now didn't he?"

Pain laced through Emma. Her parents were normally loving, kind people. They just had this awful blind spot when it came to Wayne. Sure, he'd gotten in some trouble here and there, but Emma wasn't convinced it hadn't been his way of desperately trying to get his family's attention, even if it was negative.

"They hate me," he'd told her when he was seventeen. She hadn't argued with him, even her young eyes could see the truth in the way his family treated him. "I think they've always hated me. You're the only one who doesn't, Emmy. Don't ever turn on me, okay?"

She'd promised him then, and she renewed the promise again now. She wouldn't turn on him, or on his memory now that he was gone. Wayne might have lost his way, but he wasn't the horrible loser they thought.

He was—he had been, she corrected herself sadly—still the cousin who had held her comfortingly, easing her pain over Russ, convincing her all men weren't like him, not to paint them all with the brush dipped in hot tar that Russell Barker so richly deserved.

"I don't care to have this discussion again," Emma said to her parents firmly. "I know how you feel, you know how I feel, and we've agreed to disagree."

She was amazed at how much easier it was for her to draw a line these days than it once had been. She'd been a bit sheltered—and spoiled, she admitted, being a late in life baby—by her parents, and she'd found it hard to break away. But Wayne had taught her that, too, that while you were always your parents' child, you didn't have to remain their baby unless you wanted to. It had taken her until she was nearly thirty to do it, but to her surprise, her parents had respected her determination. And now, at thirty-three, she didn't hesitate to draw that line when she needed to.

"But you're so far away," her mother said in a voice so close to a whine that Emma had to smother a laugh.

"It's a two and a half hour plane ride, Mom. Relax. It's not like I'm moving up here."

"Shouldn't be up there at all," her father muttered, but his comment had the "Okay, I'm dropping it now" tone she'd been waiting to hear. "You want me to come look at the thing for you?" he grudgingly offered. "I'll bet it's some leaky old scow that's barely afloat."

"No, Dad, but thanks. And it's floating just fine. But I'm not going to keep it, I just wanted to see it before I did anything."

"That's sensible, I suppose," her mother said, although she sounded nearly as grudging as Emma's father had.

"I'll be home soon," she promised, leaving it at that.

They loved her, she thought as she ended the connection. And she loved them. But they'd never quite let go of their little girl. Wayne had made her see they never would, and had helped her deal with that in a way both she and her parents could live with. She'd told them that they had Wayne to thank that she hadn't run from them screaming years ago, but she didn't think they believed her.

She wrenched her thoughts away from that old, well-worn path. It was time she began what she'd come here for. Despite her rather undignified beginning, she meant to finish her job here as quickly as possible and get home.

She looked around as well as she could in the light coming through the four small porthole windows. Even with her near total ignorance of boats Emma could tell that, while not quite the leaky old scow her father had called it, this vessel had seen better days. And now that she was looking around, she couldn't help wincing. Wayne had never been tidy, but this was even worse than usual.

On the shelf above the banquette where she was sitting were some books, some on sailing, some on navigation and a couple of rather lurid-looking mysteries. The rest of the space that wasn't taken up by the porthole and crushed beer cans seemed full of a pile of magazines. A quick glance at the spines startled her…Wayne had always been a gentle soul, so the stack of mercenary and hunting titles were a surprise to her. But they could belong to the previous owner of this boat, she guessed.

Next to the small built-in banquette and table was a small alcove that looked from the loose wires like it had once held electronic equipment of some sort, whether a stereo or something more nautical she didn't know. But whatever had been there was gone now, and the small table beneath was folded up and secured to the wall, one corner of what she guessed was a chart of some kind sticking out.

The kitchen—she supposed it must be a galley on a boat—was a mess. Not with food or dishes, but with a sink full and a counter covered with glasses and empty beer bottles and cans, plus the occasional empty bottle of harder stuff. She got to her feet and ventured in that direction, trying to ignore the gritty sound of her shoes crunching on what was obviously a none too clean floor.

She reached for a cupboard door and pulled, but it was stuck. She tried another, but it also refused to open. After a moment of thought, she realized they must be latched somehow, which she supposed made sense if you were at sea and things were rolling around. She shivered at the thought, but poked around until she found the small inset latch below the cupboard door that released it.

Except for a canister of coffee, some sugar that appeared to have solidified into one solid mass, and another dirty glass—this one with bright red lipstick on it—the cupboard was bare. The next was completely empty, the last held a box of dry cereal that wasn't so dry anymore.

She sighed and turned to the small refrigerator that was beside the small stove that moved when she touched it. More adaptations for seagoing, she supposed as she pulled open the door.

Beer, of course. Two shelves of it. She'd expected that, given the collection of bottles and cans. A carton of milk she didn't even dare to get close to. A piece of…something that was producing enough penicillin to vaccinate the entire marina. Cheese, maybe.

She shut the door. She wanted to stop now, but knew it would get no easier if she waited. She began to go through the rest of the boat. She started at the bow end—even she knew that much—where there was a V-shaped bunk. At least, she assumed there was beneath the large canvas bags haphazardly piled. She tugged at the drawstring on one, and saw a wadded up piece of dirty white material she guessed was a sail. There were some ropes taking up the small bit of floor, and atop them a handle or crank for something.

She backed away, then headed through the main cabin, past the disaster of a galley. There was a narrow hallway with four doors, two on the right, one on the left, then a single door at the end. She peeked into the first one on the right and found a small bathroom that looked as if it were made from one seamless piece of plastic and simply set into place; the shower head was above the toilet, and there were no seams in the floor, just a drain. Much like an RV, she thought.

The next door on the right yielded a nicely tidy stateroom with two stacked bunks, a wider one below and narrower one above. There was a small hanging closet and a couple of drawers to one side, and a large storage space beneath the lower bunk, all of which were empty, as were the shelves that surrounded the bunks on three sides. It was small but also cozy-feeling, and she instinctively began to picture it made into a personal place, with pictures hung in the few available places, and books on those shelves.

It really was a clever use of space, she thought, realizing that that was something at a premium on board a boat. She knew people lived aboard boats, and tried to picture herself fitting all her belongings on board this one. She'd never thought of herself as a particularly possession-oriented person, but the thought of what she'd have to give up disturbed her. Still, the idea of paring your existence down to the essentials had a certain appeal. It would be freeing, if nothing else, she guessed.

The door on the left appeared to be a workroom of some kind, with tools and a bench. It looked untouched. That didn't surprise her; mechanical things had never been Wayne's strong point. Which had only added to her surprise at the idea of him living on or even owning a boat that would require a certain amount of mechanical upkeep.

She closed the door and moved on to the last door at the end of the narrow hall. When she opened it and took her first glance inside, emotion slammed into her, bringing tears to her eyes in a rush.

She blinked. She hadn't expected the room—clearly the master stateroom—to be so...so Wayne. It was cluttered, Wayne fashion, with clothes and other things tossed wildly about, and the floor navigable only by careful steps. Judging by the odor, some of the things were long past needing a trip to the laundry. But there was his old favorite jacket, tossed atop a chair. A pair of worn jeans hung from a closet doorknob, and a sweatshirt adorned the top of the partially ajar door itself.

She hadn't really thought about how deeply personal this would be, how wrenching. She'd been so puzzled by the idea of the boat in general that she hadn't really thought about Wayne's personal belongings being here, and that she would have to go through them. She felt a burst of chagrin; her first thought had been to sell it, to save her struggling shelter. But it had been Wayne's home.

With a heavy sigh she looked around, and tried to decide where to start.

Tried to decide if she had the heart to even begin.

Three

——

She was going to stay on the damn boat all night.

Harlan glared at the glow of light from the portholes of the *Pretty Lady*. The boat's interior had remained unlit until well after dusk, and he'd dared to hope she'd already gone and he'd simply missed her departure. If she was gone, maybe he could stop thinking about her.

But then the lights had come on, and he'd wondered if it had just taken her that long to figure them out. He'd seen Purcell himself wrestle with the old-fashioned kerosene lamps before he'd managed to get them going. The boat had battery power, but the wiring was so old Wayne had said he was afraid to use it, and so he'd never plugged in at the dock.

Harlan had suspected there was more to it, such as the extra cost for a full hookup, but he'd figured it was none of his business. He'd spent his share of time living hand to mouth, and he knew that sometimes all you had left was your pride.

"For all the good your pride did you," he muttered to the departed Wayne.

It was such a nice evening he'd looked forward to spending it sitting outside on the deck, watching the stars, listening to the familiar and comforting sounds of boats afloat—the gentle slap of water on hulls, the distinctive soft thump of rigging and ropes in the breeze and the occasional clank of metal as a turnbuckle hit a mast. He'd grown up with such sounds, and they were as soothing as a lullaby to him.

But now, knowing the woman was over there, barely thirty feet away, and liable to swoop down on him demanding he tell her everything he knew about her departed cousin, he couldn't even begin to relax. Not that he didn't understand, but dealing with someone else's pain was more than he could stand right now. Just getting past his own was taking every bit of endurance he had, which admittedly wasn't much these days. And he had none to spare to fight off images of a sexy blue-eyed woman. One with enough curves to make him think of how warm she'd be on a winter night.

He'd been sitting in the plushly upholstered booth, leaning his elbows on the polished, high-gloss mahogany table in the *Seahawk*'s main salon when the irony of it hit him; he was acting as if he were just as much a prisoner as he'd been before Draven had come after him. The thought jabbed at him painfully, a stinging prod of that same kind of pride he'd just been ribbing the now defenseless Wayne Purcell about.

So, he said to himself in the tones of a lecture, *you either hide in here like you're still a captive, or you get your butt up top and do what you planned to do.*

It took him a few more minutes of self-chastisement, but finally he grabbed a lightweight jacket and headed outside. Determinedly he plopped himself down in the comfortable lounge that was angled to give him the best view of the sunset on Mt. Baker, and settled in for the show.

He managed to let the glorious spectacle of the sun turning the snow-clad volcano to an orange-pink he'd never seen anywhere else keep him from looking to see if the occupant of the *Pretty Lady* was visible. But as the light faded and full dark quickly set in, he finally gave in and glanced over.

The lights were still on, but there was no sign of the woman. He hoped she hadn't done any serious damage in that tumble she'd taken, something that wouldn't show up until later. But she'd seemed more embarrassed than anything, had given no indication that she'd hit her head, and a concussion was the only aftereffect he could think of that might develop.

He tried to reconcile Purcell's fond memories of his childhood companion with the woman he'd found sprawled on the floor. When he was drunk enough to talk about her, which was often, Purcell had described an energetic, adventurous tomboy unafraid to climb trees, fences or whatever it took to carry out their expedition of the day. What Harlan had seen was a petite, curvy woman with clear blue eyes and a delicate, pale complexion, the only hint of the child a stubborn chin and, of course, the other feature she had shared with her cousin, the sassy, upturned nose.

What Purcell had never talked about—at least not without a snarl of anger—was the rest of his family. And Harlan had never pried, figuring the man had his reasons. Some things took too much energy. Especially a drunk Harlan had guessed would end up exactly as Wayne did. Cold, he said to himself even as he thought it. Cold, but anything more was simply beyond him. Like now. He felt a mild curiosity about Emma Purcell, but that was all.

His brow furrowed as he realized that even mild curiosity was more than he'd felt for what seemed like a very long time.

"Mr. McClaren?"

He nearly jumped. That was new, too, being so lost in thought that anyone could sneak up on him. He'd spent most of the last few weeks hyperaware of every little noise, as if he were still surrounded by threats.

He looked in the direction of the voice, not that he needed to, he knew who it was. She wasn't embarrassed now, so that undertone was gone, but he sensed about the same level of tension, and wondered why. After a moment he worked himself up to responding.

"Ms. Purcell."

An expression that appeared to be part relief and part acknowledgment crossed her face, visible even in the faint light that remained where she stood on the dock beside the steps. From where he was, he was looking down on her slightly; at eighty feet the *Seahawk* was a big boat and she rode high on the incoming tide.

It didn't register until then that she'd called him by name, although he'd never given it to her. Again he was only mildly curious, but also again the sensation was something unfelt long enough to be noticeable to him.

"May I speak to you for a moment, Mr. McClaren?"

"Harlan, please," he said, deciding at almost the last second, for reasons he wasn't sure of, not to give her the nickname most people used, Mac. "Is it getting to you?"

"Emma," she returned, almost mechanically, he thought. "What do you mean?"

He glanced over at the *Pretty Lady*. "She's never going to make the cover of *Boat Beautiful*. And Wayne wasn't much on housekeeping."

"He was always messy."

Bet it wasn't always beer cans and booze bottles, though, Harlan thought, but kept the words to himself. Far be it for him to pass judgment on how someone chose to deal with the pain in their life.

"That wasn't what I wanted to talk to you about," she said.

"I never thought it was." He stifled a weary sigh. This was what he got for being determined not to let her stop him from what he'd wanted to do, he supposed. "You might as well come aboard."

She hesitated, looking at the *Seahawk* as if it were some sort of alien spacecraft she'd been invited onto.

"Or not," he said after a moment. "I guess I can yell down to you, if you don't mind the rest of the marina hearing every word."

That did it, as he'd suspected it would. She came up the boarding steps, although he noticed she did so very carefully. He got up and held out a hand to help, but she either didn't see it or ignored it; he guessed probably the latter.

Once Emma stepped on deck, he guessed because she felt the solidity of it beneath her feet, she seemed to relax a little. He'd left a light on inside the main salon, and he saw her glance at it. He knew it looked like a room in any well-furnished home, spacious and comfortable, and she seemed to relax even more.

He studied her face for a moment, and decided that

had Josh gone in for the ostentation others did in boats this size, she wouldn't have relaxed as much.

He gestured her toward the empty lounge chair opposite him, then stopped. "Unless you're too cold to stay outside?"

"No, I'm fine."

He shrugged. "Always check with you California folk."

She frowned. "What makes you think I'm from California?"

He turned on the outside fixture that flooded the deck with light. "The tan?" he suggested, looking pointedly at her pale skin as he resumed his seat.

She blinked at that. He smiled, indicating the joke. She got it. Gave him a halfhearted smile. Sat down.

"Your cousin was, so I assumed," he said.

She ignored his explanation and said abruptly, "I want to ask you about that last night."

"Cut right to the chase, don't you?"

"This is very important to me. You said you saw Wayne an hour before."

She still couldn't say it, he noted. Nearly a month and she still couldn't use that word of ultimate finality.

"Before he died?" He said it pointedly; his patience for avoidance tactics had been left in a cellar in Managua. "Yes, I did. About an hour before they found him floating facedown over there."

He finished with a gesture toward the *Pretty Lady,* and Emma looked. She turned back to him, her eyes wide, her complexion even paler than before. Harlan saw her tighten her lips, as if to keep a cry or a sob from breaking free. And he suddenly felt like an utter heel, for being so cold to her.

"Look, I'm a little tired. I'm sorry I said it like that."

She didn't look as if she believed him, but she didn't linger on it.

"Was he really that drunk that night?"

His forehead creased. "Didn't the police tell you?"

"They told me what his blood alcohol was. What I'm asking is if he seemed that drunk to you."

Harlan shifted uncomfortably in his seat. "How he seemed to me doesn't mean anything. I've known guys twice as drunk who acted sober, and half as drunk who couldn't function."

"But if he was that drunk and acted sober, how did he fall into the water?"

He was beginning to feel beleaguered. "I didn't say he wasn't drunk. He always was."

She stiffened at that. Harlan bit back more sharp words.

"When was the last time you saw him?" he asked.

"In person? Three or four years. But we spoke regularly, up until…" She stopped, clearly thinking, trying to remember. Then her mouth twisted slightly as she finished. "Until he came up here, I guess, judging by the timing."

He held up his hands. "Don't blame me. I've only been here a few weeks."

"I wasn't blaming you," she said, a little too quickly.

So, you've at least wondered if I had something to do with it? he said to himself. "He was well down the path he was on when I showed up," Harlan said.

"And what path was that?"

He shrugged. "I don't mind other people's business."

"Maybe if you had Wayne would still be alive!" she snapped.

He said nothing, because there was nothing to say.

He couldn't even deny it, because it may well have been true. And he wasn't about to explain, because an explanation would require him to tell her why he had so little to do with other people, and he was nowhere near ready to talk about that.

"I'm sorry," Emma whispered, her eyes lowered and her voice shaky. "I had no right to say that."

He shrugged again; he'd found it a useful way to acknowledge something without actually having to commit himself to speech.

"It's just that…" Her voice trailed off, and he saw then that her hands were clasped so tightly together her knuckles were white. After a moment she looked up at him. "Wayne was like my brother. We were the only kids in our entire family near the same age. We played together constantly in those days. He was so adventurous, so eager to explore and learn. We had wonderful times. And then when we grew up we were…confidants."

He could have said that they weren't as close as she'd thought if she didn't know how serious his drinking problem was, but he held back. He didn't want to feel like he had a while ago, like he'd tromped on some fragile, rare flower.

"I tried to support him in his fights with his parents, and he held me together when my engagement ended nastily."

There was an undertone of pain in her voice, and he found it telling that it was no worse when talking about her own problems than her cousin's.

"What about your parents?" he asked, surprised at the effort it took not to ask about that ended engagement.

She blinked. "What?"

"They were his aunt and uncle, right? Was he…how did you put it? Was he dead to them, too?"

She looked decidedly uncomfortable. "They didn't get along much better," she finally admitted. "My dad tended to agree with Uncle Jerry about Wayne. Mom tried, but she gave up, too."

He didn't say anything, but something must have shown in his face, because she spoke quickly, with words that sounded as if they'd been used before. Often.

"I know what it sounds like, that everybody in my family thinks Wayne is a loser but me, so I must be wrong. But he isn't, not really."

He is now, Harlan thought, but again didn't say it. He also didn't comment on her use of the present tense. The realization that he was not saying so much was a bit startling to him. Usually nothing popped into his head to say or not say. Was this perhaps a sign he was finally coming back to life? Not sure if he welcomed that idea or not, he tried to concentrate on what she was saying.

"—just a little confused about what to do with his life, that's all."

"Most people have that figured out by his age," he said.

"Most people don't grow up with their parents telling them they can't ever do anything right," she retorted, an edge in her voice.

"So you think he lived down to their expectations?"

"I know he did. He told me more than once that if they were going to hate him anyway, he might as well enjoy it."

His lips curled before he could stop it. And when she looked at him questioningly, to his surprise he found himself answering the look.

"My mother," he explained. "Before she died she always used to tell me I was going to end up as feckless as my father."

"So you understand!" she exclaimed.

"I could have gone that way, I suppose," he said. But instead, he'd been determined to prove his mother wrong.

"That must be why Wayne liked you," she said. "He sensed you knew what it was like."

That was far too esoteric for him. "I don't think he liked me so much as I was convenient," he said. "And," he added wryly, "I had an icemaker."

"You make it sound like all Wayne ever did was drink!"

He resorted to the shrug yet again. "I can only say what I saw. Maybe you'd be happier not hearing it."

Emma said nothing for a long, tense moment as she studied his expression. Finally she said, "You think I'm blind and naive."

It wasn't really a question, and Harlan guessed that was because she'd said it to herself more than once. Which meant she likely already knew the answer. She obviously had no idea what her cousin had really been like, or how he'd apparently changed since she'd last seen him. And he'd clearly kept a lot from her.

He wondered what Emma Purcell would say if he told her everything, how many times he'd seen Wayne return to his boat too drunk or stoned to walk, how many times he had fished the man out of the water himself. Or if he told her about the odd comings and goings of some very suspicious-looking characters on the *Pretty Lady,* and about the arguments he'd heard coming from belowdecks, between her dead cousin and a man who reminded Harlan far too much of the men who peopled his nightmares.

But he wouldn't. Wayne was dead, and there was no point in destroying the image of the one person who had apparently thought well of him.

"I think you loved him, and we're never eager to hear that the people we love have made bad choices." His voice gentled. "Especially when it's too late to change anything."

Tears welled up in her eyes. *Well, that does it,* he thought. He'd been as gentle as he knew how, and he'd still made her cry. That hadn't changed, it seemed.

"Sorry," he muttered. "I always manage to tick women off one way or another."

"I'm not angry," she said. "I'm hurt."

He winced; that was worse somehow.

"The truth does that, sometimes," she added, her voice steadier now. She stood up. "And you were right, it got to me. Not the mess, just the realization that this was what became of Wayne's life. He could have been so much more."

She turned her back on him and started toward the steps. She stopped before she stepped off the *Seahawk* and onto the stairs leading down to the dock. She looked back at him.

"Thank you for talking with me."

He watched her go, wondering if she'd lumped him in that "could have been more" category as well. And feeling a little twitch of unease as he realized that it mattered to him, for the first time since he'd been here, what someone else thought of him.

Four

Emma was exhausted. When she'd retreated to the sailboat she'd been so filled with conflicting emotions she'd wanted to strike out at something, anything. She wanted to break something, wanted to hear it crash. And that was a feeling she'd rarely had in her life. She didn't like it.

She was angry. At Wayne, for first dropping out of her life, then back in by forcing her to deal with all this. At herself, for being so hurt by what was being shoved at her. And illogically, at Harlan McClaren for shoving it.

Which was what she'd like to tell him to do, she admitted now. Except that she wasn't sure enough he was wrong to say it.

If she had to judge by this mess, everything the man had said was likely true.

I can only say what I saw. Maybe you'd be happier not hearing it.

There was the crux of it, she supposed. She *would* have been happier not hearing it. What that said about her she wasn't sure. Nor was she sure she'd like the answer.

"Damn you, Wayne," she whispered. Then she said it louder, then louder, until she was yelling it.

And then she was doing exactly what she'd wanted to; she picked up one of the dirty glasses and flung it wildly. It hit a wall and then the floor, but bounced unsatisfyingly. She picked up another and heaved it with more intent, toward the base of the mast that ran through the cabin. This time it shattered, and the sound helped ease her coiled up emotions. But it wasn't enough, and she threw another glass, then another, until a little voice in the back of her head started talking about having to clean it up. Then she knew she'd taken some of the edge off, and she stopped.

The hatchway swung open, startling her. A man stood there, peering in.

"Are you all right?"

Harlan McClaren. Running to her rescue for the second time in one day. She felt her cheeks heat, and hoped he couldn't see her color in the dim light.

"Haven't we played this scene once before?" she said, trying to hide her embarrassment to being caught in her temper tantrum.

"Yes, but without the extra sound effects," he said. "The breaking glass ones."

"Ah," she said, with a wave of her hand she hoped looked blasé. "I thought it needed something extra."

She thought she saw one corner of his mouth twitch, and hoped he was buying her light tone. This time he only brought his feet in, just far enough so he could sit on the top step. Whether it was to stay farther away from possible flying glass or to save energy—he had admitted he was tired—she wasn't sure. But when she saw him studying the small pile of broken glass at the base of the mast, she spoke quickly to avoid any embarrassing questions.

"I still can't get used to the idea that Wayne left me a boat when he knows I don't like the water."

"So you said," he said, in a tone that said he couldn't imagine that being true.

"Some people don't, you know."

He gave a sharp shake of his head, as if to clear away the ridiculousness of that. "That's hard to believe, for somebody who grew up on the water."

That caught her attention. "You grew up on a boat?"

"Not one. Several different ones. But yes, since I was seven. I've never lived on land for any length of time. It makes me nervous."

"If I was a little calmer, I'd be only nervous about being on a boat," she retorted.

But despite herself she was interested. Just as she'd be interested, she told herself, if she met someone who lived on a volcano, or in Antarctica.

"That must have been an unusual life. How did you go to school?"

"I didn't."

Emma gaped at him.

"At least not in the traditional sense," he amended. "We were never in one port long enough."

"You mean you sailed from place to place?" Had he really been a marina bum his entire life?

He nodded. "It was the best education a kid could

get. I had to learn local customs in a hurry, and how to get along with all kinds of people. Languages, too.''

She stared at him, knowing her astonishment at this kind of life, especially for a child, must show. But she was unable to help it when what he was saying was as foreign to her as living on the moon would be. She tried to focus on the one thing he'd said that made educational sense to her.

''Languages, plural? How many do you speak?''

He shrugged. He did a lot of that, she'd noticed. ''I'm fluent in four or five, I can get by in a few more and can find the bathroom or food in about a dozen more. All the necessities.''

In spite of herself she was smiling, for the first time today. But she couldn't help asking, ''But what about other things? Reading, math, science?''

For a moment he hesitated, and she had the startling thought that maybe he didn't—couldn't—read. She'd seen lots of books in her quick glance inside the big boat, but those could easily, in fact likely did belong to the boat's owner.

''My dad taught me what I needed to know.''

She understood now. He was a marina bum because he couldn't do or be anything else, with no higher education or even a high school diploma, it seemed. She thought of how the chrome and brass on the boat he was living on gleamed, how the decks were spotless, and there was none of the rundown appearance the *Pretty Lady* had. Perhaps he did work for his keep, although if she had to guess, she'd say the *Seahawk* was out of any price range mere work could pay for.

When she came out of her thoughtful reverie, he was studying her in a way that made her nervous. She wondered how much of that was due to her growing and unwilling fascination with this man.

"You went to college, I assume?" he asked, in a tone that made her even more nervous.

"Yes." She started to give the name, as was habit when people asked, because it was usually the next question. But mentioning Stanford seemed pretentious just now, so she didn't.

"Master's?"

"Not yet," she said. "I was working on my MBA when something else came up."

"Don't tell me you quit school for some guy and got married?"

She let out an explosive little chuckle. "I wouldn't stay with a man who would want me to give up my dreams just to marry him."

"Good for you," he said, then looked as if he wished he hadn't. Hastily, he stood up. "Well, if you're all right," he began, glancing at the broken glass once more.

"I will be," she told him. "I just wish I understood."

"Understood?"

She gestured around her. "Why Wayne did this. I don't even understand why he bought this old thing anyway. He never seemed interested in boats before."

She knew Harlan had been on the verge of escaping, and she felt the need to stop him, this man who had possibly been the last one to see Wayne alive, and certainly one who had seen more of him than she had in the last days of his life.

"You said he talked about me." She spoke quickly, out of her need to keep him here. "Did he say anything about this? About leaving it to me?"

Slowly, still standing on the steps and clearly reluctant, he turned to look at her. "You're really puzzled about that, aren't you?"

She grimaced. "I'm surprised he even had a will, at his age. Wayne wasn't one for planning for the future."

"Maybe he—"

He stopped himself so abruptly Emma knew that whatever he'd been about to say was likely something she wouldn't want to hear. And while she didn't really trust this man—or rather, didn't trust her judgment about men in general—Wayne had trusted him, and so decided he was probably right and let it go.

"I am puzzled," she agreed. "He knew I didn't like the water, or boats. So I wondered if he'd said anything to you that might explain it."

He didn't answer right away, which told her he knew something. If Wayne had said nothing to him, the "no" would have come easily.

"Please, Mr. McCl— Harlan. Wayne was a little wild, I know, but he had reason. And I really need to know his reason for leaving me this boat."

With a tired-sounding sigh and moving so slowly he looked as if he were in pain, he sat back down. Suddenly flustered, Emma began to jabber.

"I'd offer to fix you coffee, but I'm not sure how old it is."

"I'm not sure I'd trust any of Wayne's utensils anyway," Harlan said wryly, and she couldn't argue with him. "You might as well come over to the *Seahawk*."

She shook her head, more in response to the continued reluctance in his tone than his words. "I don't want to impose, just because this isn't as…nice."

"Then how about because I'm afraid it'll sink?"

Some joke, she thought as her stomach instinctively tightened. He was joking, wasn't he? She glanced around warily, half-expecting to see the hull spring a leak under her gaze.

"Relax," he said, apparently relenting. "I was kidding. It's not going to sink. Not immediately, anyway."

She grimaced, all her old fears about boats rising up with renewed force. "How can you be sure?"

"I dove the hull for him. It's got problems, but nothing that's going to drag her down in a hurry."

"Is that what you do? Dive on boats that need repair?"

"When I'm not diving for treasure." It sounded like a joke, so Emma concentrated on the more important question.

Should she trust him? she wondered. Wayne had said she could. But could she trust Wayne's assessment if he was as far down the road to ruination as it seemed? Maybe he'd only said it because Harlan was a drinking buddy. Although she had to admit, she'd seen no sign yet that he was drinking. Of course, she'd only been here a day.

"You going to sleep aboard?" he asked.

Startled, she shifted her gaze from the boards beneath her feet back to his face. "I...I don't know. I hadn't thought about it. I thought I would find a motel somewhere close by."

He lifted a brow at her. "Good luck with that. Only thing in town is three times as old as this boat, and more rundown."

She frowned with all the puzzlement of someone from Southern California where anything you wanted was usually a block away. "Surely there must be something newer around."

He shrugged, only one shoulder this time, and she wondered if the other was tired of it. "To the south, in

Poulsbo, there's a couple. Twenty minute drive in good conditions.''

She looked around at the interior of the boat again, this time with an even more critical eye. Could she stand to actually stay overnight on a boat? More particularly, on this boat?

She suppressed a shiver. Or thought she did, but apparently not well enough.

''You weren't kidding about not doing boats, were you?''

''No.''

''Come on, then. On the *Seahawk,* you can forget you're on one, if you want to. Then you can decide what to do.''

She hesitated, but only for a moment. She couldn't think rationally here, and she knew it. She did want to forget she was on a boat. And she could control this silly reaction she had to him. So when he got up, she followed.

He had to be out of his mind. Simply and purely nuts. What on earth had he been thinking, inviting her into his only sanctuary? Sure, she'd looked terrified at the idea of spending the night on the *Pretty Lady,* but that didn't mean he had to play the happy host.

Well, he'd get this done, tell her what he could—or at least what he felt she needed to hear—about her cousin and then send her on her way. Back to the boat, or off to some landlocked motel, that was up to her.

He told her to take any seat in the salon, then stepped into the small galley. The main galley was down one level, where there was room for a chef to prepare a gourmet meal for one of the business meetings Josh occasionally conducted aboard. Up here were just the basics; a small fridge, microwave, ice maker and the necessities for snacks and drinks.

"Wine? Beer? Champagne? Something stronger to make the *Pretty Lady* more palatable?"

She looked at him as if she wasn't sure he was kidding. She tended to look at him like that, which made him think his efforts at humor were weaker than he'd thought. Probably because his heart wasn't in it. He wasn't sure his heart was in anything anymore.

"No thanks." Then, with a sideways look she asked, "Do you offer champagne to every casual visitor?"

He wondered if she was thinking he was trying to make a move on her, then decided it was more likely she was thinking he was giving away booze that wasn't his. "To the guy who owns the boat, no visitor is casual."

"He sounds like quite a guy."

"He is." Not wanting to get any deeper into that, he checked the fridge and asked, "How about a soda?"

"If you have anything without caffeine, that'd be fine."

He nodded and pulled out two cans.

"You don't have to have that because I am," she said.

"Figure you're keeping me from my nightly binge?" he asked as he set the soda down beside her seat.

She had the grace to blush. "No, I just meant..."

"Never mind," he said when her voice trailed away. "It was a natural assumption. But just for the record, your cousin could drink me under the table without even breathing hard."

She went very quiet then, and he felt another jab of guilt at tarnishing her image of her cousin. She sat running a finger over the plush seat cushion as if trying to figure out the fiber content of the material.

When he sat down across the low table from her, he had to take a deep breath just to start. The effort it took was far more than it should have been, but he'd grown almost used to the simplest things taking every ounce of energy he had. And in this one day he'd already expended far more than usual by this time of the evening.

"Wayne said you were close as kids."

She nodded without looking up. "I told you. Like brother and sister."

"I meant proximity," he said.

"Oh. Yes, we lived close, so we spent a lot of time together." After she'd spoken she looked up, seeming only now to realize the implications of what he'd first said. "He talked about us?"

He nodded. "He talked about you...regularly." *Any time he got drunk, which was every night,* Harlan thought, but kept his mouth shut this time. He'd done enough damage already in that arena.

"Did he say anything that would explain this?"

Get it over with, and get your space back, he ordered himself. "He told me one night that he was going to leave it to you if anything happened to him, yes."

"But why?" she asked. "Why a boat?"

"Because it was all he had."

She blinked. "But there's his town house in San Francisco, and his cars. He collected them, classic cars."

Damn. How had he ended up doing this for that drunken sot? He'd barely known him, and he didn't know this woman at all, there was no way he should be doing this. But there didn't seem to be any way out of it, and Harlan grimaced before he spoke. "He told me he lost the house some time ago. And he sold off the last car years ago. He was broke."

Her eyes widened, then narrowed. "That must be why he changed to a post office box in San Francisco. He said it was because his building was being remodeled."

So, he did lie to her, too, Harlan thought. He'd wondered if perhaps there had been one person Wayne had never lied to. He should have known better.

But it was clear he wasn't going to get past this blind spot of hers easily. And he simply didn't have the energy to push the issue until she saw the truth. It was none of his business anyway, even if he did have some desire to force her to open her eyes to the real person her cousin had been.

"But...what happened?" she asked. "He had it made, with that Internet design business. He'd finally proved them all wrong."

He didn't figure he needed to point out that Wayne also hadn't had a computer in over a year. And unless she absolutely cornered him, he wasn't going to tell her his suspicions about where all that money had gone. Hurriedly he searched for a distraction that would head off any of those questions.

"Proved them wrong?" he asked, even though he already knew who she meant.

"His parents," she said, her voice tight. "And mine, too, for that matter. They abandoned him when he was fourteen."

"Didn't the law have something to say about that?"

"Oh, I don't mean literally abandoned, as in kicked him out when he was still underage. They would never do that, but emotionally they cut him off completely."

"Sounds pretty extreme."

"They said he got into trouble once too often, but really, he was just a little wild. He never deserved that from them. I love my family, but I hate them for what they did to Wayne."

"That explains it, then," he said before he thought.

"Explains what?"

He wished he could call it back, but it was too late now. Resigned, he related to her what the drunken Wayne had told him. "He said he was going to leave the *Pretty Lady* to you because you were the only one who would care if he died."

Five

"**O**h, God," Emma whispered, and her eyes began to fill with tears. *How awful, to have to say that only one person in the world would care if you died,* she thought.

She lowered her head and stared at her hands. "How could they do that to him?" She'd asked herself countless times before, but now it seemed the most urgent question in the world. She lifted her head to look at Harlan through the tears, not even caring that she was weeping in front of him. "How could his own family turn on him like that?"

He hesitated, as she'd noticed already he often did before speaking. But finally, with another of his fatalistic shrugs, he said, "I gave my dad reason to give up on me more than once. But he never did. And on some level I think I knew he never would."

"And how different would your life have been if you

hadn't known that?'' she asked softly. ''If he had given up on you after some stupid prank or a little trouble.''

''I don't know how to answer you,'' he said finally. ''Who can tell someone else how much they should take?''

''But when it's your own son....'' She shook her head.

''Maybe Wayne crossed too many lines for them,'' he suggested.

She opened her mouth, then closed it again when she realized she'd been about to repeat herself.

''If your own parents agreed,'' he began, and stopped.

''I don't understand that, either,'' she said. ''They're not unfair, generally. And I know they wouldn't have blamed him just for losing all the money he made. My dad's had some tough business times.''

''Obviously it was more than that.'' His voice sounded as if he were keeping it determinedly neutral.

Her brow wrinkled as something else occurred to her. ''If he was broke, how did he buy that boat? Even in the shape it's in, it must have cost something.''

Harlan rubbed at the back of his neck, as if the muscles were tight. For her, that kind of tightness warned her of an impending headache.

''He said he had a windfall. An inheritance. So he bought the boat.''

She frowned. ''An inheritance?''

''He said it was from an uncle who'd died.''

She blinked, now utterly confused. ''What?''

''That's what he told me. An uncle had died and left him just enough to buy the *Pretty Lady*.''

''But that's impossible,'' she protested. ''The only

uncle he has is my father. Who is quite alive and kicking.''

Harlan looked at her steadily, silently, letting the obvious speak for itself. She couldn't deny it. Wayne had lied yet again.

Her emotions began to boil up, until she knew she had to be alone. Her practical mind on autopilot, she went through the motions of thanking him for talking to her, for the soda, all the while fighting down the riot within.

She was vaguely aware of him asking, for the third time on this hellish day, if she was all right. And for the first time she gave him an honest answer.

''No. But there's nothing you can do about it.''

''Been there, done that,'' he said softly, and to her relief, let her go.

This time the dim interior of the *Pretty Lady* was exactly what she needed. Unlike the *Seahawk,* where the room they'd been in was above the deck, on the *Pretty Lady* the main cabin was below, which gave it a cavelike feeling. And a cave was exactly what she needed right now. A cave where she could curl up and simply ache, like some injured wild creature.

She sat down on the threadbare banquette, and drew her legs up until she could wrap her arms around them. She rested her chin on her knees and sat there staring, seeing nothing of what was really in front of her, just a chain of vivid images of the boy she'd loved as a brother, and the man she now wondered if she'd ever known at all.

And so it began, Harlan thought. Emma Purcell had had the first bit of reality about her beloved cousin tossed undeniably in her face. He wondered what she would do. She spoke of him as if he were still the boy she'd grown up with, a bit wild, perhaps, but basically good.

Harlan had the feeling Wayne Purcell had left "basically good" behind him some time ago. In the days before his death, Harlan had wondered if something was going on, because Wayne had been unusually edgy. Even after his usual several rounds of beer or booze, he'd seemed agitated, tense, and he would pace the floor unsteadily. On most nights when Wayne showed up at the *Seahawk,* he was already noticeably stoned or drunk, and his mood ranged from bitter to maudlin. But those last few nights, if he had been high he'd been so wired it didn't show.

Or, Harlan amended wryly to himself, he'd just changed his method of intoxication to something more revving.

He tried to focus on the computer screen in front of him, but the world that had so fascinated him for years now left him feeling only a casual interest. When coupled with the vague restlessness that had suddenly overtaken him, the combination had him rather unsettled.

It was just a coincidence, he told himself, that this feeling had begun today, just when Emma Purcell had dropped into his life. They'd told him he'd go through stages like this, times of uncertainty about his life and whether he could ever go back to what it had been. Stages when new things would draw him, and that that wasn't necessarily bad, as long as he realized he couldn't erase what had happened by tearing his entire life down to the ground and building a new one.

Emma's gentle, sweet, kind and caring, Wayne had said. And while he might well have been right, there was a touch of fire there as well, Harlan thought. There was a pile of broken glass aboard the *Pretty Lady* as proof of that.

He wondered if, had Wayne been around, she would have heaved those glasses at the cousin who'd lied to her and everyone else. At what point did the childhood images finally fall away?

"There are none so blind," he muttered, and turned back to the computer screen, ordering himself firmly to put Emma and her problems out of his mind because they were just that, her problems, not his.

He had enough of his own.

Emma woke with a start. She hadn't been aware of falling asleep at the table, but at some point she had laid her head down on her backpack and that was it. The cabin was filled with light from the portholes, and a quick glance at her watch told her it was early morning. So early it surprised her that it was so light, until she remembered how far north she was, and figured out that the sun really did rise this early in the summer.

It was already warming up in the cabin, although she suspected it could get quite chilly at any other time of the year. In fact, judging by the cold tip of her nose, it had gotten colder than she was used to last night.

Emma was a doer by nature, and deciding activity would be the best thing to warm her up, she got to her feet. She wasn't up to figuring out the intricacies of the valves and levers of a boat bathroom—a head, she supposed—just yet, so she went up the dock to where she'd seen a set of bathrooms. Once she'd handled that and splashed some water on her face, she walked quickly back to the *Pretty Lady,* glancing at the *Seahawk* and noting it was still quiet.

Everything was quiet, she thought. She was so used

to the constant barking at Safe Haven as newcomers adjusted and old-timers warned of anyone's arrival, that this unending peace was a novelty. The only regular noise was the atmospheric sound of ferry whistles and other boats as they traversed the sound.

To her surprise, she found it all almost pleasant. This morning the sound was so peaceful and quiet, like a sheet of barely rippled glass, and being on the water hardly bothered her at all.

It must be fascinating to live here, she thought. Which was a major step for her; until now the very idea would have sent her running. But this morning she could see the appeal. Maybe this really could be a vacation for her. She supposed she could even overlook the presence of Harlan McClaren, although she had to admit that for all his scary appearance, he'd been quite nice to her. Yes, she thought, nice. That was a good word. A safe word. That it didn't fit with the quickening of her pulse every time she saw him was something she chose to ignore.

Back aboard the sailboat, she began by cleaning up the mess of broken glass she had made. Then she turned to face the rest. She had to clean it up, she reasoned, even if she was going to sell it right away. It would bring more money if it was clean, and Safe Haven needed all the money she could get. But for a moment her spirit quailed; it seemed like an insurmountable task. Then she stiffened her spine, set her jaw and began.

She couldn't find anything resembling a trash bag that wasn't already full, so she commandeered a large cardboard box that held ropes of various lengths. She dumped them out for sorting later, and began to toss the empties into it. By the time she'd cleared the sink and small counter—plus added the cans from the bookshelf—the box was full. She dug around under the sink until she found a ragged sponge and a quarter-can of cleanser which was, she judged by the solidity of the contents, probably left over from the prior owner of the boat. A few slams against the counter loosened up enough powder to dump some in the stainless-steel sink. The tap produced a thin trickle of water, but it was enough for the task.

It took her the better part of the morning but finally she had the main cabin to where she could stand to look at it. It took her two trips to get the trash up the dock to the Dumpster. She sorted the cans into the recycle bin, then brought the empty box back, figuring she'd need it for the rest of the mess. She'd lose some weight at this rate, at least.

She tried to concentrate on the job at hand, but it was too routine to require all of her attention, so much of her mind was free to think about things she didn't want to, like Wayne lying to his own family.

To her.

He'd never lied to her before. At least that she knew of. As kids, no matter what his wild plan, he'd told her about it. Sometimes she was able to talk him out of it, but unless he was going to get hurt or arrested, she generally didn't try. And no matter what trouble he'd gotten into, he'd told her afterward. Sometimes she agreed with him that he'd gotten a lousy break, sometimes she didn't, and when she didn't she'd told him, but it hadn't affected their relationship. And she had never told on him, so he had never stopped talking to her.

She thought about the bragging he'd done about his town house in San Francisco, how much fun he was having with his little fleet of cars. He'd told her that one day he'd come back and take her for a ride in the Ferrari down Lombard Street.

But he'd told Harlan the truth about his losses, apparently. Just not about where the money to buy this boat had come from. So why had he confessed the rest, but lied about that, and to a man he'd only met a few weeks ago?

She didn't like any of the answers she came up with to that question.

Figures, Harlan thought. I finally get to sleep and the phone rings for the first time in two weeks.

He sat up, ignoring the protest of his still aching shoulder, and shook his head to clear it before picking up the receiver.

"Yeah," he muttered, stifling a yawn.

"Still not sleeping at night?"

Draven, he thought. He'd never forget that voice. The voice that had been the harbinger of his salvation, belonging to the man who had led him out of hell.

"Not well," he admitted. *But not just for the reasons you probably think,* he added silently.

"Pills?"

"Trying to avoid them."

That quickly he adapted to Draven's habit of reducing speech to the essentials.

"Pain?"

"Some. Getting better."

"Doctor?"

"Not for another month. Barring problems."

"Dreams?"

Draven's tone didn't really change, but Harlan knew it wasn't a casual inquiry. This was a man who had demons of his own, a man who knew what it was like to bottle them up all day only to have them erupt at night when your guard was down.

"Oh, yeah," he said, knowing Draven would understand.

"They'll fade, Mac," the voice said, and Harlan knew the words, saying only they'd lessen, not go away, were chosen intentionally.

"I figured I'd picked up a lifelong passenger."

Draven didn't deny the truth of that. "Need anything?"

"I'm on the *Seahawk*. What do you think?"

The chuckle pleased him; not many made Draven laugh.

"Tell me," he asked, "do you always take such a personal interest, or are you following up for Josh?"

"Josh takes care of his own."

Another patented Draven answer within an answer, Harlan thought as the call ended with the same abruptness. He'd learned a lot about the man he'd only heard of before his Nicaraguan expedition had turned sour, and one of the things was that he never gave anything away. He supposed it was a necessity in the man's line of work; when you saw as much mayhem as Draven had, a thick shell would be the only thing that enabled you to keep going.

He'd also learned it did no good to lie to the man; he had a built-in detector that seemed infallible. The first time he had called Harlan tried to tell him he was doing fine, almost good as new. Draven had then enumerated every kind of nightmare and haunting he was battling before ending with "…but other than that you're fine, is that what you mean?"

He'd never tried to bluff the man again.

But that didn't mean he told him everything, he

thought as he made his way up into the main salon. Like not telling him that one of the reasons he hadn't slept was the woman digging her way through the rubble her cousin had left her. He'd encountered other women since his rescue, but no one who had edged her way into his consciousness like Emma had. He wasn't sure why she'd gotten through to him, and somehow admitting it aloud would make it more real.

It had to be the personal connection, he told himself. He'd known Wayne—as much as anyone could know a drunk on a few weeks' acquaintance—and had heard a lot about Emma before he'd ever met her. True, she hadn't been quite what he'd expected. He'd somehow gotten a picture of a plain and very loyal woman, a sort of girl next door type with bookworm tendencies. The woman who'd shown up here might be a bookworm, was admittedly loyal, and was literally the girl next door just now, but in no way would he ever call her plain. Not with that sassy nose, full lips, those eyes, and those curves.

He would add determined to the description, he thought as he poured himself a cup of the coffee he'd made earlier. From behind the safety of the tinted windows he'd watched her make a couple of trips up the dock with a big box loaded with Wayne's debris. It was about then that he'd made himself head back to his bunk, because he was feeling the urge to offer to help. He didn't want to help. Didn't want to get any more involved with her than he'd already become, simply because he'd had the misfortune to be a convenient place for her cousin to drink and vent.

He'd done the best he could. He'd answered her questions, tried to do it without totally destroying her image of her cousin, so now he would withdraw. What she did from now on was her business. Maybe he could finally get her out of his head.

But he spared a silent curse for Wayne Purcell, wherever he was, for all the damage he'd done.

After three days this life was beginning to grow on her. She'd gotten through that first night well enough—albeit unintentionally—that she decided to try sleeping aboard, in the one tidy stateroom. After an hour or so of getting used to the unusual sounds, the clanking of rigging, the lap of water, the occasional sound of a distant engine or horn, and a little longer to get used to the incredible quiet beyond those sounds, she had gone to sleep soundly. She had awakened with amazement that she had slept so well, and after a little thought had decided she would save the money she would have spent on a motel and stay here.

The very idea would have made her laugh just days ago, but she was now beginning to understand the lure of this life. She still doubted she would ever come to love the ocean, but this inland sort of sea was something she could live with.

She barely felt uncomfortable anymore when she walked along the docks, less than a foot and a half above the water. It was the sound, she decided. It was the ocean, and yet not; it had none of the things that made her uneasy. And she found it unexpectedly peaceful in the mornings when the water was so calm it was glassy, and the sky looked like a vivid watercolor painting.

Her focus was still on cleaning out the mess that was Wayne's boat, but she caught herself more than once stopping to simply look, soaking up an atmosphere she would never have expected to appreciate at all. It made even her worries about Safe Haven recede a bit.

She hadn't seen Harlan at all, and was irritated with herself for how often her mind went to him, wondering where he was.

Wondering if he's avoiding you, you mean, she chided herself. Because she had wondered. And then wondered why it mattered. Despite his helpfulness in their meetings until now, she was still a little afraid of the man, with his haggard looks and haunted eyes. But she was becoming aware that there was more to it than that, although she didn't want to admit to a fascination that had little to do with fear.

So this time, when she walked back to the boat after another long trip up to the Dumpster, she picked up her pace and forced herself not to even glance at the *Sea-hawk.* And as a result, nearly knocked Harlan off the dock. He grabbed her as she careened off of him, saving them both from a tumble. He was, she realized, stronger than he looked.

And eyelashes, she thought. He had incredibly long and thick eyelashes. The kind that made you think of how they would feel brushing your skin.

She was staring at him. Hideously embarrassed she tried to think of something to say, but he saved her.

"You look like a woman with a mission."

"I am," she said, grateful to him for not noticing— or at least not saying anything—about her gaping at him. "I'm trying to clean up this mess." She gestured in the direction of the *Pretty Lady.*

He seemed to be wrestling with something before he said, "I'll leave you to it, then."

He turned to go. She wouldn't stop him when he

clearly was anxious to get away, but she did want to ask something.

"Could I ask you something?"

He stopped, and for a moment stood with his back to her, as if he were fighting not to turn around.

Or fighting to make himself turn around, she thought, wondering where the idea had come from.

At last he did, and said simply, "What?"

"Do you know anyone here who knows about sailboat stuff? I've got a pile of ropes and clasps and things that I know nothing about, and some of it may be important."

Again that pause while he pondered his answer. Or, she thought, getting that odd feeling again, whether to answer at all.

At last, almost resignedly, he said, "I know a bit. I'll take a look."

"I don't want to take you away from…whatever you were doing," she said quickly. "I just thought you might know someone."

"I'm not doing a thing," he said, with an emphasis that made her wonder what he'd read into her hasty words.

He walked past her without a word, not even looking to see if she was following. If he'd meant to make her feel like she was imposing, he'd succeeded. She thought about just telling him to forget it, but decided since she did need somebody to look at that stuff and tell her what she needed to keep, she'd just let him do it, and then hustle him out to go back to whatever it was he did.

"Wow."

The exclamation came from him the moment he stepped down into the cabin. It warmed her, after all

her efforts. When she'd made her way down the steps—
safely now, after several trips—he turned to look at her.

"You've been busy," he said.

"Cleaning was the only thing I could think to do,"
she admitted.

"It makes a big difference." He leaned against the
back of the banquette and looked around. "It wouldn't
take much more to get this looking good in here. A little
sanding here, tighten up some hinges, patch that ding
there. Throw in some reupholstering on those cushions,
replace the electronics and you're in good shape."

"Good enough to sell?"

"Is that what you plan to do?"

"What else would I do with it? I know this isn't the
Seahawk, but just from what I've seen, the upkeep has
to be expensive."

"They say a boat is a hole in the water into which
you pour money," he agreed. "Which reminds me.
Have you been to the marina office yet? I don't know
how far in advance Wayne paid the guest docking
fees."

That hadn't even occurred to her. "Well, if they take
over the boat for back payments, that solves my problem," she said glumly.

His mouth quirked. "Since it's only a few dollars a
week without power or water, I doubt that." His expression changed, became serious. "But don't be surprised if he didn't pay much. He was dodging the manager the last couple of weeks, and I'm guessing that's
why."

"He didn't even have enough money to pay that?"
It was more a rhetorical question than one really expecting an answer. And he took it that way, responding
with his characteristic shrug.

With a sigh she turned back to the matter at hand. She led him to the workroom where she'd been collecting all the items that looked like they might play a part in sailing, or at least be a part of the boat itself.

"I just tossed anything that looked like it might be important in here. Oh, and all the ropes."

"Sheets."

"Excuse me?"

"Sheets. On a sailboat, the lines are sheets."

She blinked. "Then what are the sails?"

"Sails. The line attached to the mainsail is the main sheet. The jib, the jib sheet. And so on."

"What's a jib?"

"The sail that goes in front of the mainsail. Although a spinnaker does, too."

Emma shook her head. "Never mind. It's all beyond me."

"Don't figure you want to learn enough to take off for a round the world cruise?"

She shivered at the idea. "I've come a long way in the last three days, but not that far."

"Give it time," he said. "It grows on you."

"Maybe," she said. And silently she admitted that she never in her life would have imagined herself saying anything but "No way" in answer to that statement.

He began to sort through the things she'd set aside. The ropes first—he put them all in the "save" pile she'd set aside. "You can never have too much," he explained. Then he tossed several metal clasps into the box as well, for the same reason, he said. Next he picked up three pieces of twisted metal, and glanced at her.

"I didn't know," she said. "They looked just bent, but I thought maybe they had some purpose."

"They were brackets once, but never will be again," he said, and tossed them into the bag she'd set out for trash. Then, to her surprise, he leaned down and out of the bag pulled a handful of what she had assumed were useless short lengths of colored, thin plastic about the consistency of a balloon.

"Wind gauges," he said, transferring them to the save box. "You tie them on stays for wind direction."

His voice was merely explanatory, so she tried not to feel stupid for having thrown out something useful.

He picked up the big silver metal handle she'd found. "I guessed it has to turn something," she said, "but I have no idea what."

"Probably your mainsheet winches, judging by the size."

"One handle for both?"

He nodded. "You only use one at a time, port or starboard."

"Oh." She'd felt totally ignorant at other times, but never more than now.

The winch handle went into the save box. Followed by two odd-looking metal things he told her fastened sails to halyards, whatever those were. Then he picked up a strange piece of metal that had looked to her like one of the things that were up on the cockpit railing, a heavy silver cylinder about the size of a big juice can, only with concave sides.

"Odd," he said as he turned it over and looked at the bottom. Or the top, for all Emma knew.

"What's odd?"

"This winch is light," he said.

It had seemed heavy enough to her, but then she had no idea how much something like that should weigh.

He apparently spotted something on the side now

turned upward. He looked closer, then reached toward the center with two fingers. He tugged at something that was jammed into the hole in the center of the cylinder, what looked to her like an old rag. After a moment he had hold of the edge of it, and tugged it free. Something else fell to the floor as the rag came out, and he bent to pick it up.

It looked to Emma like a simple piece of paper, rather intricately folded. And given the condition of the rag, cleaner than she would have expected. Harlan stared at it for a moment, then began to unfold it with a care she didn't understand.

When he was a couple of folds into it, he held it up closer to his face. And to her surprise, he wet the tip of his little finger, touched something inside the fold, and tasted it. He grimaced, but wryly, as if whatever he'd been curious about, he'd just had his suspicions confirmed.

And suddenly, like a video taken by her mind, the things that had just happened in front of her played back in her head, and at last she saw the significance of actions she'd seen in countless movies and police dramas.

"Oh, God," she murmured. He looked up at her then, and she saw the truth in his eyes. "Drugs?" she asked, although in her gut she already knew the answer.

"Cocaine."

Six

"**I**'m no expert," Harlan said, "but that's my guess. I thought he might be into something more than booze, but he hid it well. But I guess that explains where the navigation gear went. He probably pawned it."

The loose wires in the main cabin, she thought numbly. She stared at the little folded up paper as if it could bite her. Then she looked at the cylinder that had held it, and which, to her horror, she could now see held at least one more of the little packets.

"I'm sorry, Emma."

His voice was soft, more gentle than she would have guessed it could be.

Still staring at the grim evidence that Wayne had been in worse shape than she'd ever imagined, she muttered. "It's not your fault."

Or is it?

She wasn't sure where the idea had come from, but

there it was, fully formed, trumpeting in her head like a warning, too late for Wayne but not for her.

Were those tired eyes not the result of some illness or injury, not the world-weariness of a man who'd seen too much, but instead the reflection of an evil soul who led others to destruction? They were, she had to admit now, the kind of eyes she'd always imagined a drug dealer would have, sometimes haunted and sometimes blank and cold. But she'd seen pain there, too, and surely someone who dealt in such things wouldn't feel anything like that? When you dealt in death, surely you lost any sensitivity about it.

She was looking at him with new eyes, feeling as if she'd been wearing blinders all this time and now they'd been ripped off. His thinness…didn't addicts get skinny? Maybe that was it, maybe he wasn't a dealer, but simply an addict who had sucked the suggestible Wayne into his nasty world. Misery loves company and all, maybe he just hated to get high alone. Maybe that was why he sometimes seemed so reluctant to even talk, why he always seemed anxious to get away. He didn't want anyone to look too closely and realize he was high or stoned.

Stop it, she ordered herself. *He's here helping you, that's all he's really done since you arrived, and you're making a whole lot of wild guesses based mainly on his looks.*

''You're saying it's not my fault, but lady, your eyes are yelling the opposite.''

He'd read her so accurately she was startled first, before embarrassment that he'd guessed what she was thinking about him flooded her. She felt pinned by his gaze, a steady and direct look that made her doubt all her suspicions. How could a guilty man look at her like that?

Then he turned his back on her and finished the sorting job rapidly, pointedly minus the explanations he'd been giving. He worked rapidly, giving each item a minimal inspection before making the decision to keep or throw away. She was so surprised that he'd elected to finish the job at all that she just stood there watching, figuring the best thing she could do now was keep her mouth shut.

When he tossed the last piece into the save box, he dusted off his hands and turned around. "Whoever you sell her to will likely know what they are," he said, his voice inflectionless as he gestured at the save box.

Without another word he moved past her, careful not to come too close. In the doorway he stopped, and looked back over his shoulder at her.

"There's a fine line between loyalty and blindness," he said.

Then he walked out of the workroom. She heard him go up the steps to the deck. She stood there for a very long time, staring at the silver cylinder.

He'd left the damning evidence there, and she wondered what on earth she was supposed to do with it. She certainly didn't want to get caught with it. Not that the police were likely to make a raid here. At least, she didn't think so, but then again, if Wayne had been living a secret life she knew nothing about, if he'd gotten so lost he'd resorted to drugs....

She knew so little about the realities of such things. She knew they existed, she'd had acquaintances in college who had experimented with various things, but she'd been working too hard to keep her scholarship to risk such things, even if she'd been so inclined.

There's a fine line between loyalty and blindness....

Was she? Was she really blind about Wayne? Were his parents and her own right, had they been all along? Or was Harlan just declaring himself innocent of her suspicions? Was he telling her she was looking for a way to absolve Wayne from responsibility and hang it on him?

Slowly, she walked out of the workroom and across the narrow hall to the stateroom she'd been using. She went to her purse and dug out her Dayrunner, then flipped to the small pocket she hadn't looked at since the day she'd gotten the call about Wayne.

She hesitated before she took out the first picture, steeling herself. It had been taken in much happier times, during a summer day spent at the mountain lake their families often visited together. It was of both of them sitting on a sun-drenched rock, smiling into the camera with the impatience of kids ready to get on with the play and only humoring their parents by staying still long enough for this shot.

"They didn't hate me yet," Wayne had said when she'd showed it to him shortly after she'd found it in a box of old pictures the last summer they'd had together before differing paths pulled them apart.

"When did they start?" she had asked, not disputing his claim since she'd seen too much evidence of it herself. "What happened?"

"You think I haven't asked myself that a hundred times over? I don't know. I mean, sure, I get in a little trouble now and then, any guy my age does." He'd looked at her then, with an odd expression she hadn't understood. "I should hate you, you know."

"Me?" She'd been beyond startled.

"I've had you thrown in my face for as long as I can

remember. 'Why can't you be more like Emma?' 'Emma would never worry her parents like this.' Emma, the perfect child, the perfect girl, the perfect teenager, just all-around perfect.''

''I'm glad you don't hate me,'' she'd said, but she remembered thinking then that if they really hated him they wouldn't be worrying about it, but before she could say that Wayne had been on to something else.

There's a fine line between loyalty and blindness....

She reached in for the second photo. Wayne's high school senior portrait, a shot which did little to conceal his anger and turmoil. The set of his jaw, the tightness of his lips, the flash in his eyes screamed it. She stared at it for a very long time, wondering what she'd missed.

Or what she'd refused to see.

It hit him hard that night. Harlan never knew what would set it off, and never knew afterwards what had. But there it would be, a night when he wished he had never even tried to sleep. A night filled with haunting images and terror and memories of hideous pain.

That his predicament had been his own fault made it even worse. After years spent navigating in dozens of uncharted backwaters, of finding his way into bays and coves no one had ever taken a boat into before, he'd made a simple—and nearly fatal—wrong turn on land.

He awoke this time as usual, in a sweat, his T-shirt soaked, his sweatpants damp. It was almost routine by now; he rolled out of the bunk, peeled off his clothes, and headed for the shower. After a rinse cold enough to make him gasp he toweled off, resisting the urge to check and see if the scars were fading, pulled on a pair of jeans, grabbed a shirt and made his way up to the main outside deck. The air was cool on his bare chest, and finished the job of bringing his body temperature back down to tolerable levels.

It was a full moon. He shivered suddenly, and pulled the shirt on. It had been a full moon when he'd been caught, and the memory of the silvery light turning his captors to demons of the night never left him. Ever since, moonlight had made him edgy.

But in that light, he easily found his way to the lounge chair at the back railing of the deck. Purposefully he picked it up and turned it so that its back was to the *Pretty Lady*. He didn't want to think about that— not even wanting to say her name in his mind—right now. He couldn't deal with his own unruly response to her. Not now.

So instead Harlan sat and stared up at that full moon, willing his body to relax. He wished his mind was as easy to control. But he'd never learned the knack of thinking about nothing, and nothing he did try to think about was strong enough to distract him from the lingering fog of his nightmares. The odd thoughts of the wife and fiancée who had walked out on him—no, he'd driven them away, he amended fairly—were easier to take than this.

A movement up on the marina bulkhead drew his gaze. It was a woman, unmistakably, her body ripely curved and graceful as she walked. Her hair gleamed in the silver light, showing him her head was lowered as she watched either the water or where she was walking.

Emma.

Well, maybe one thing was strong enough to distract him, he thought wryly.

What *was* it about her? She'd practically accused him of being somehow involved in her cousin's drug use. Maybe even of being his supplier. Not that she'd said it, but her suspicions had been so clear on her face he'd read them like he read the stars at sea. He supposed he couldn't blame her, she didn't know him at all, she was probably still in shock over the death of a cousin she'd loved, whether he deserved it or not. In a way, he even admired her loyalty, even though it had led her to some very wrong conclusions.

But he still found himself thinking about her—or trying not to—more often than not.

It wasn't simply long abstinence. He'd frequently had the chance to end this bout of celibacy, especially among women who knew who he was, but he hadn't felt even the slightest flicker of desire to do so.

At least, he hadn't until now.

It was ridiculous. From everything Wayne had said Emma was a devout homebody, while he wandered the globe. She was the girl in the house next door, while he'd never lived in a house at all. They had absolutely nothing in common.

Of course, he thought as he watched her walk down the dock toward him, he wasn't sure things in common were a requirement. It wasn't like he had anything in mind more serious than he ever had. A girl in every port, that was the best way for a guy like him, always moving on, following the wind.

Had been, anyway. Even that seemed to have lost its appeal, lost it in a damp, dark cellar in a Nicaraguan jungle that civilization had never reached.

He wondered if he should get up and dodge into the shadows as she passed. He certainly didn't want to deal with any more of her accusations, and after the exhausting nightmares didn't have the energy to defend himself anyway.

That thought made him wonder what she was doing

up at midnight, walking around alone. Not that she was in any danger here in this quiet place, this county had a crime rate that would make Southern California laugh—or sigh with longing. She could probably—

A sharp sound snapped his head around. He stared through the night, wishing for the first time the already bright moonlight was brighter. He glanced back at Emma as she passed him, her head still down. And then back to where the sound had come from.

The *Pretty Lady.*

Maybe she had company, he thought. But then why would she be out walking around by herself?

No further sounds came from the sailboat, so he stayed where he was and watched as she headed up the dock stairs and then stepped onto the deck. She headed into the main cabin, and he watched as she disappeared below, never having even glanced his way.

He sat back down, wondering exactly when he'd stood up. Maybe this was some weird stage of recovery the shrink hadn't warned him about.

With a sigh he gave up on any idea of more sleep tonight.

He'd been there. She'd been careful not to look, but she'd sensed him there as clearly as if he'd been spotlighted. As he no doubt would have been by the flood of moonlight.

She concentrated on going down the steps into the main cabin as if she was as unsure of them as she had been the first day. It didn't help much, there was still too much of her mind free to think about the man aboard the *Seahawk.*

She told herself he was so in the forefront of her mind because of Wayne, because she wanted to know what

he might have had to do with the downward spiral
Wayne had apparently been in before his death. But she
wasn't having much luck convincing herself that it was
only that.

Okay, she said to herself as she reached the bottom
of the stairs and was confronted by the few piles of
papers—everything from pages torn out of a phone
book to a few scribbled phone numbers on napkins—
that were on the table for her to finish sorting through.
Okay, she repeated silently, admit there's something
about him that appeals to you, something behind the
sometimes frightening look, beneath the reluctance that
seemed to be there so often.

Suddenly even those few papers to sort seemed overwhelming. She wondered if she would finally be able
to sleep. It was worth a try, she decided, and turned to
head down the narrow hallway to the stateroom she'd
been using. She'd been sleeping fine, somewhat to her
own amazement, up until tonight. But the discovery of
those paper bundles hidden away had thrown her completely, and she was still trying to deal with it. She
didn't know how to do it, didn't know where to put this
bit of unwanted, unwelcome knowledge in her image of
Wayne. She didn't know—

A hand came out of the darkness and grabbed her
from behind.

Seven

She screamed in the instant before the hand covered her mouth, which she guessed had been his original intention but he'd missed. She recoiled at the taste of skin, then grabbed the opportunity and bit down. Hard.

"Ouch! Bitch!"

The voice was low, harsh and definitely male. Moreover, it was not Harlan's, which had been her thought in the first split second.

She'd startled her attacker, and her gut told her she'd better take advantage of it. She drove back and up with her elbow, made contact with something soft that produced a sharp "oof" out of him, then something harder she guessed was a rib.

He swore again, and his grip loosened. She twisted with all her strength and managed to pull free, but he grabbed her arm. Desperately she looked around. The only thing in sight was the broken barometer hanging

on the wall. She grabbed at it and swung as hard as she
could at his head. Connected. It splintered, barely stag-
gering him. But he howled. She turned to run.

"Nick, what the hell's going on out there?"

Her heart sank. There were two of them.

His heart hammering in his chest as he leaped, Harlan
cleared the rail of the *Seahawk* and came down on the
dock, skipping the steps completely. Emma's scream
was still echoing in his ears, and he dreaded what he
would find when he got to the *Pretty Lady*.

He didn't bother to try and sneak—whoever or whatever it was, he wanted them to know help was coming.
He belted down the steps into the main cabin, thankful
she hadn't locked up for the night or he never would
have gotten in short of using an ax. He barely noted the
main cabin was a mess all over again as he plowed
through the debris, toward the noise at the stern.

He didn't know just what he'd feared he would find,
but what he saw wasn't it. A man lay sprawled in the
hallway, obviously stunned. Emma, it seemed, was
tougher than she looked. And then he heard another
muffled scream. He glanced swiftly around, wishing
he'd grabbed something he could use as a weapon from
the *Seahawk* before he'd jumped ship. He couldn't see
anything, and knew he couldn't waste any more pre-
cious seconds.

He ran down the hall, leaping over the man sprawled
there. He was beginning to stir, but so slowly Harlan
guessed he had a small margin there.

He heard a thud from the workroom. Then a low
curse just as he made it inside. Her assailant had his
back to the door, and Harlan took only a split second

to notice the man had Emma by the waist, and that she was making him fight hard to hold her.

"Come on, let's get the hell out of here!" the man exclaimed, obviously thinking Harlan was his downed comrade.

"Good idea," Harlan said, grabbing the winch handle he'd tossed in the save box. "Let her go."

Startled, the man jerked around. Emma twisted violently in an effort to get free. Harlan didn't waste any time waiting to see if she really would break the man's grip, he swung the winch handle. The odd shape made it difficult to aim and the spinning handle was hard to control, but it connected with enough force to make the man grunt. As Harlan had hoped, the man released Emma, who stumbled to her knees. But the man quickly turned on him.

He came in low and hard. Harlan braced, but knew the man outweighed him by at least thirty pounds. And he had little faith in his strength just now. Speed, he thought. It was all he had left. That and fighting skills learned on the docks of the world, in many a backwater port.

At the last second Harlan took a quick step to the side. He raised his right knee hard and fast. Caught the man under the jaw. His head snapped back and he went down.

Emma was on her feet now. Her gaze flicked to the man on the floor, then up at Harlan, her eyes wide. Something flickered in them, and he knew in the instant before she cried "Behind you!"

He spun, crouched and launched himself before the man who'd been down in the hallway got into the workroom. He slammed him up against the wall with his full weight. The man's knee came up, driving hard. Harlan

dodged, and jammed a forearm against the man's throat.
The gurgling sound he made echoed in the tight quarters. The man swung at him wildly. Harlan head-butted
him, bloodying the man's lip.

"Damn you!" the man shouted.

"You're too late," Harlan snapped. In the same instant he heard a scraping sound from behind him. The
other man was getting up, charging. He dug his shoulder
into the belly of the man he held against the wall.
Kicked out behind him with his right foot. Connected,
hard, the impact sending a jolt all the way up to his hip.
The man went down again.

But the man against the wall was batting, clawing at
him. Twice he struck the still tender spot on his back.
The pain was making his head reel. He hadn't been in
a fight like this in a long time.

Then the man on the floor began to come up again.
And Harlan knew he was still too weak to take them
both. But then Emma was charging toward them, wildly
brandishing the winch handle he'd managed to drop.
The man on the floor took one look at her and her
weapon, and scrambled down the hallway, using his
hands in a desperate effort to get fully to his feet.

Harlan felt a searing pain in his right upper back as
the man he was trying to hold struck again. He'd sensed
the weakness. Harlan's right arm slipped, and the man
jerked free. He shoved hard. Harlan grunted as he
slammed against the opposite wall. Thankfully the man
didn't linger but followed his companion, and seconds
later they heard the clatter of feet going up the steps,
over the deck, and running footsteps as the men hit the
dock and escaped.

Harlan felt himself sliding down the wall, his legs
giving out. He hit the floor with an ignominious thump.

He tried to steady himself, tried to take in some deep breaths, but he wasn't having much luck. And then Emma was crouched beside him.

"Are you hurt?"

How could he answer that? Yes and no? I am, but it was a long time ago, not now? Six months ago I could have taken them both, I swear?

His silly words spun in his head. At least she wasn't hurt, was all he could think that made sense.

"Your back is bleeding!"

It was? That startled him enough to slow the spinning.

"I'll call for the paramedics," she said, and began to get up. He tried to speak, couldn't, and settled for grabbing at her arm. She looked back at him, and he shook his head. "But you're hurt," she said. Then frowned. "He didn't have a knife or anything, did he?"

She was wondering why he was bleeding. A question he wasn't about to answer. So when he finally found the breath to speak he said only, "It's not bad. It'll stop."

She frowned. "Well, at least let me look at it."

He shook his head. Another deep breath and the words came more easily. "I'm fine. Or I will be."

"But you got hurt helping me. The least I can do is take care of it."

His mouth quirked. "Judging by the way that guy took off when you came after him, I'd say you didn't need much help."

"I can protect myself, but I could never have handled two of them. Thank you."

He didn't feel he'd done anything worth thanks, so said nothing. He moved his legs tentatively. They were feeling better. He pulled them up under him and, using the wall to brace himself, was able to stand. He was very aware of Emma watching him, and pushed away from the wall as soon as he could. It wasn't just her, he told himself when he realized what he was doing. It was anybody. He hated the idea of anyone seeing him in the shape he was in, not just Emma.

He refused to think about the fact that he was failing utterly to convince himself of that. But some part of him, the part that had been honed down to the essence in his captivity, knew the truth. That Emma was getting too close.

And he was letting her.

Harlan started down the hall, looking for the first few steps as if he half-expected to fall on his face. Still worried about the blood she saw seeping through his shirt, Emma followed him. She stayed close enough to grab him if her interpretation of that look was accurate. If he was aware of her behind him it didn't show, and he didn't stop until he reached the main cabin and slowly sat down on the banquette.

"You'd better call the police," he said.

She blinked, startled. "The police?"

His forehead creased. "To report this," he said. "Are you all right?"

"I'm fine," she said hastily, although she was still feeling more than a little bruised and shaken. "It's just—"

She stopped herself when she realized she'd been about to ask him if he was sure he really wanted her to call the police out here. But he'd suggested it immediately, and without any sign of concern about them coming. Surely he wouldn't be so ready to involve them if he were really a drug dealer?

But if he wasn't, then what on earth was he? Where had he learned to fight like that? Not that she'd ever seen a fight like the one that had taken place in that hallway in person before, down and dirty and two against one, but it didn't take an expert to realize Harlan McClaren had fought like that before. Probably often, judging by the way he'd handled himself. If he were in top shape, she didn't doubt he could have handled both of them. Easily.

"It's just what?" he asked.

"I don't have a phone book here," she said rather lamely.

"I think this would rate a call to 9-1-1," he said wryly.

"Oh. Of course."

She made the call, found out it would be the sheriff, not the police, and gave what information she could when they asked for descriptions of the two men. After assuring the efficient dispatcher that no medical help was needed—although she still wasn't completely convinced about Harlan—they went up top into the night to wait.

She felt safer up here in the moonlight than she had in the dimly lit interior of the sailboat. She'd meant what she'd said; she'd taken classes and learned how to defend herself from an attacker, but two of them with the advantage of surprise had been far more than she could handle.

She smothered a shudder as she remembered the terror that had filled her when that hand had come out of nowhere and grabbed her. She sat on the roof of the cabin next to the boarding stairway.

"Are you sure you're all right?" His voice was gentler now, as if he'd seen her reaction to her thoughts.

She took a deep breath and steadied herself. It was over now, she was fine, it was time to buck up, as her father always said.

"I am," she declared. Then added with a wry grimace, "Except for the chaos."

"You mean that?" Harlan asked, gesturing back toward the inside of the cabin with his thumb. She nodded. "How long were you gone?"

"A couple of hours, at the most. I stopped at the marina office to pay the back docking fees, then went to get some food." She hesitated, then realized she had no choice but to ask him, "Will you do me a favor?"

"If I can," he said, in the cautious tones of a person wary of what he was about to be asked.

"I don't want to tell them about the drugs."

His brow went up. "But isn't that likely what those guys were after?"

"That's what I thought, at first," she said.

"You didn't still have them, did you?"

She flushed. "I didn't get rid of them," she admitted. "I didn't know what to do with them."

"You want my advice, dump it overboard."

And surely an addict wouldn't say that, would he? she asked herself. Wouldn't he offer to "get rid" of them for her, take them off her hands so he could use the drugs himself? Quickly she looked away from him, afraid he'd read her suspicions in her eyes.

"I don't have the stuff now. They found it." She looked at him then, feeling under control once more. "That's why I don't want to mention it. They found and kept the drugs. But they also kept looking." She sighed and finally voiced her fear. "They were looking for something else."

"Maybe they were just looking for more dope."

She shook her head. "They talked about it. One of them said after they found the packets that that wasn't what they were here for and to keep looking."

"Keep looking for what?"

"I don't know."

"Well, where were they looking?"

She gestured in turn to the cabin. "You saw the mess they left. They were looking everywhere. Tearing out drawers, tossing stuff out of cabinets."

"Did they look inside things?"

She frowned. "Inside? They looked in the packing boxes, if that's what you mean."

"What about inside jars, or smaller boxes?"

"No. They looked in books, though," she said thoughtfully, only now realizing what that told her about the size or shape of what they'd been hunting. "What could be hidden in a book? Unless it was one with some pages hollowed out. But how would they know to look for that? And how—"

She broke off when he held up his hand. "I don't know. Papers, a ledger or, as you said, something small enough to be hidden there. Or maybe directions to where something else is. No way of knowing."

Headlights at the top of the dock caught her eye, and she suddenly realized he'd never really answered her. "Are you going to tell them?"

"They should know there are drugs involved."

"But we don't know that they're directly involved in this. And Wayne's dead, so…"

Her voice broke on those last words. He hesitated, then sighed. "All right. For now."

Relieved, she nodded. "Thank you."

And she thought how ironic it was that she was thanking the man she'd more than suspected of being an evil companion to Wayne, leading him astray, and then supplying him with drugs. And now he was the one only reluctantly agreeing not to tell the sheriff's deputy now on his way down the dock about the now missing drugs. And despite her own words, she wasn't at all certain this break-in hadn't been related to those drugs.

An image hit her suddenly, of that day Wayne had warned her she wouldn't find peace in the bottom of a bottle. Obviously, he'd been speaking from experience, she thought bitterly. So underneath all that wondering was the one big question she wasn't sure she wanted answered. What kind of man had her beloved cousin become?

Eight

"Let's get this cleaned up."

Harlan did mean to help. She'd worked hard, and all her efforts had been destroyed in the space of a few minutes. Now that he had time to look, he could see that the cushions had been slashed and the stuffing pulled out, cubbies pried open, pictures and charts ripped off the walls and smashed on the floor. No place that could have hidden something small and flat had been overlooked.

But he also wanted to keep moving. He had a nasty feeling he was going to stiffen up as soon as he stopped.

"You don't have to—"

"Let's just do it, all right?"

She looked at him for a moment. "If you'll let me clean up your back first."

He stiffened. He'd forgotten about that. There was no

way in hell he wanted her looking at him. "It's fine, really. I'll take a hot shower later, get the shirt loose."

She looked at him for a long moment, then her mouth quirked. "Somehow I'll bet that's not up in the community shower."

The image of the *Seahawk*'s bathrooms—far too luxurious to be called just heads—popped into his mind, and he couldn't stop a grin from breaking loose. It felt strange, and he realized it had been so long he'd forgotten what it felt like to use those muscles.

"No," he agreed.

He hadn't thought about that. Wayne had been roughing it, no electricity or water on the *Pretty Lady,* because he didn't have the money to pay the extra charges. Or didn't want to spend it on that instead of booze.

And dope, he thought. Too bad she had to find his stash that way.

"Let's get this done. Unless you want to wait until morning."

"No," she answered quickly. "I don't want it like this. I couldn't stay here." She shivered. "But I don't think I can anyway."

That played on his mind as they worked. They spoke only to coordinate the job. She attacked the mess in a very organized manner, top down, she said, so that cleaning up the things that were irreparable off the floor would come last. She worked methodically and continuously, until Harlan ruefully had to admit to himself that just now, she could work him into the ground.

Although weary when they finally finished, Harlan was warmed up and moving easily except for the slight twinge from his back, and he wondered if therapists had ever considered housework as exercise. He surely felt like he'd used every muscle group he had. Emma, on the other hand, simply stood and surveyed the results with a satisfied expression.

He stifled a yawn and glanced at Emma's watch—he'd stopped wearing his the day he'd caught himself looking at it five times in ten minutes—noting as he did that for a strong, healthy-looking woman, she had a very delicate wrist.

It was nearly two in the morning. Recalling how she'd shivered at the idea of staying where she'd been attacked was still vivid in his mind, and he couldn't blame her. How could he, when the place he'd been chained and tortured haunted his nightmares regularly?

Emma finished her perusal and nodded, so he guessed they were done. Then she turned to him.

"Thank you."

He shrugged. "No problem."

"I really do appreciate the help, especially with all that fingerprint dust all over the place."

"Maybe they'll get lucky," he said. Emma had cleaned so thoroughly before the break-in that the crime scene investigator thought that once they eliminated hers and his own, they just might have some good ones. Which, he thought, was odd.

"I wonder why they didn't wear gloves?" she asked, vocalizing his silent question.

He shrugged; she wouldn't like any of the answers he'd come up with. Another yawn snuck up on him, and he couldn't stop this one. She caught the urge and yawned in turn.

"I'm sorry this kept you up so late," she said.

"I'll sleep in."

The faintest of creases appeared between her brows and he knew she was thinking of sleeping here again. And with a sigh he gave in to the inevitable.

"You might as well move over to the *Seahawk*."

She blinked. "What?"

"You sure don't want to stay here, at least not for a while, and it's a bit late to head out and try to find a motel room."

"But—"

"You've got your choice of staterooms, a bathroom next door, and lots of hot water for a long, private shower." He nearly laughed, and did smile at the expression that crossed her face then. "I see I should have started there if this was a sales pitch."

She had the grace to laugh at herself. "It showed, huh?" She sighed. "Well, maybe for tonight, at least."

"Grab what you need and head on over. And lock up," he added.

She paled. "You think they'll come back?"

He shrugged. "I doubt it, but you never know."

That, he saw, vanquished any last reservations she had. "I'll just get some things," she said, and turned to go.

Then she turned back, just as he had taken a step forward, and she came up practically against his chest.

"I just wanted to say thank you." She said it quickly, but breathlessly.

Like I'd sound if I tried to talk right now, with her so close, he thought, having to work to drag in enough air for his next breath. It was a mistake; he caught the scent of her, warm and womanly, and his body charged to attention.

Just say "You're welcome," he told himself. Then she'll go.

He didn't say it. He tried, but the words simply would not come. It was as if her closeness had stolen his ability to speak at all.

It had also, apparently, planted the stupidest question he'd ever thought of, in his mind.

What would she taste like?

Which followed by the stupidest idea he'd ever had. Kiss her and find out.

He didn't know what had shown in his face, he only knew she turned and vanished quickly down the hall and through a port-side doorway.

Now you've done it, he thought.

He'd just single-handedly destroyed his own fragile peace of mind.

To Emma's surprise, after the shower that was everything he'd promised, she went to sleep quickly, and slept soundly. The new surroundings, she guessed. The new and obviously safe surroundings; Harlan had shown her the sophisticated alarm system that protected the *Seahawk.* She woke up rested, looked around and added luxurious to the list of descriptors.

She stretched expansively, enjoying the much larger bed. And bed it was, not a built-in bunk like she'd been using on the *Pretty Lady.* The entire stateroom was as far opposed to what she'd been in as a five-star hotel was to a tent. The fabrics were rich, the wood warm and polished, the fittings gleaming gold. And the bathroom...

She'd never realized you could have marble and a Jacuzzi tub on a boat. But there was that and more, down to a heated towel rack that had seemed both the height of decadent luxury and the most wonderful thing she'd ever used.

Harlan had told her this was one of the smallest staterooms on the *Seahawk,* but it was hard to believe. The second bedroom in her apartment wasn't much bigger. Not that that was saying much, she admitted.

She sat up finally, reluctant to leave her warm cocoon of comfort, and wondering if she could steal a few more minutes of wonderful sleep. She glanced at the clock bolted to the bedside table, not to prevent theft she'd finally figured out, but to keep it from sliding away at sea, a thought that still gave her the shivers.

For a moment the time didn't register, simply because she couldn't believe it. But there was no denying what the glowing numbers said. Still, she grabbed her watch off the nightstand as if it might somehow say something different. It didn't.

And she should have called Sheila yesterday, she suddenly remembered. She leaned over and grabbed her cell out of her tote on the floor and pushed the speed dial button for Safe Haven. Sheila answered on the first ring.

"That's okay," she said when Emma apologized, "as long as you're having a great time."

"It's been…interesting," she said. "I'll tell you about it when I get home. What's happening there?"

"We're still at eight. Our lowest population in months."

"Good," Emma said. Less animals meant less food, and less work for Dr. Burke, who already donated more time to them than she had to her own veterinary practice before she'd retired. "Any calls?"

"You got two from animal control—follow-up, they said, not new tenants—and one from Mr. Weisman, who won't take it from anyone but you that Foxy's all right. Eve Hendrickson wants to know when we can bring Sweetie to visit her. The mail's on your desk. I haven't had a chance to sort it yet, except to pull out the bills.''

"I'll deal with them when I get back. Anything else?''

"Cedar Glen called, about the dog therapy program. They're willing to talk about it.''

"Wonderful! I'll get back to them as soon as I can.''

Emma meant it. She'd been working with the administration of the nursing home to allow regular visitations by Safe Haven's resident day-brightener, Whisper. The gentle, loving collie brought more smiles and cheer to a sometimes grim existence than anything Emma had ever seen. Patients in hospitals or long term care facilities brightened the moment Whisper turned those big brown eyes on them, or plopped her chin on their knees for a long, soulful look, begging for a pat on the head.

"Maybe I should head back early,'' she began, "talk to them now, while—''

"Don't you dare, girl. You're on your first vacation since you started this place.''

"That's only been two years,'' Emma pointed out.

"Two and a half,'' Sheila corrected. "And believe it or not, there actually are people who believe in taking a vacation every year.''

"I don't need a vacation.''

"Like heck you don't,'' Sheila said sternly. "And now's the time. Charlie and I can handle five dogs and three cats with our eyes closed. Who knows when we'll be this empty again? Don't you dare show up back here.''

As she disconnected, Emma had the feeling Sheila really would be upset with her if she came back now. So maybe she wouldn't. But she couldn't stay here, in the lap of luxury, the whole time. Could she?

The very idea of going back to the dilapidated sail-boat made her grimace. The thought that those two men might return while she was there made her cringe.

She got out of bed and dressed hurriedly in denim leggings and a long-sleeve T-shirt, wondering all the while what Harlan must think of her, sleeping until noon. She dragged a brush through her hair, glad yet again for the simple bob that suited her. She did the best she could with her face in a rush job, which meant washing and putting on a little mascara, and then she pulled on her shoes.

Once she stepped outside her door it took her a moment to figure out which way to go, and the novelty of a private boat so big you could lose your way on it was not lost on her. She made a wrong turn, passed several closed doors and one open one, to a room just a bit smaller than her stateroom. That room seemed filled with computers, printers and at least two fax machines, all alive and humming. But at last she found her way back to the main salon, Harlan had called it. He was there—not surprisingly, given the time—a can of soda at his elbow on the glossy galley table and a magazine spread open before him.

She stopped abruptly. He looked so…normal. None of that ominous shadow was present in the man before her. He looked simply like any guy—albeit a good-looking one—enjoying a soda while he read a magazine on…she instinctively looked at the page he had open and saw an article on some kind of private airplane at about the same level of luxury as this boat. She wondered if his rich friend had one of those, too.

Her appreciation of the pleasant tableau faded a bit,

but she chided herself. *You're just worried about money, and wishing Safe Haven had a benefactor with this kind of cash.* Besides, she thought, she didn't know if she'd turn down a chance to live on a boat like this herself.

That she would even consider it startled her a little; this place was working some odd sort of magic on her, despite the bad things that had happened since her arrival.

She opened her mouth to say good morning, realized it didn't apply, and switched to simply, "Hello."

For an instant he froze, as if too startled to move. But when he looked up she saw nothing like that in his face. In fact, the smile he gave her was the warmest she'd seen from him, and it surprised her; she'd been expecting him to have withdrawn as he had before, as if he were sorry he'd allowed her to invade his space.

But this morning—afternoon, she corrected herself again—it was different.

"I don't usually sleep this late," she began.

"I'm surprised you're up now, as late as you got to bed."

"So did you," she pointed out.

"But I had a bit of a nap before your guests arrived."

"Oh." She grimaced at the memory. "How's your back?"

"Fine," he said, with a casualness that seemed a bit forced to her. "There's coffee brewed, there on the counter, or soda and lemonade in the fridge. Bagels or cereal is about the gamut of the menu without actually cooking something, I'm afraid."

She shook her head. "Just coffee's fine. I ate late last night."

He nodded, left her to pour it herself, which she liked, and nudged a chair out from the table for her with his foot. She sat down, her gaze drawn outside to where a foggy morning appeared to be giving way to the sun.

"I thought it was supposed to rain here all the time."

"So did I," he replied. "Hasn't yet. It spit a little one day, but not enough to count."

She sipped at her coffee; it was a rich brew that warmly tickled her sense of smell as well as her tastebuds. She barely stopped herself from letting out a sigh.

"Thank you for the shelter," she said at last. "I wouldn't have slept a wink if I'd stayed over there."

She got a one-shouldered shrug on that one, and she considered adopting the handy, nonverbal, fits all situations answer.

"Not to mention the shower," she added. "It was luscious."

He smiled at that. Then he got a quizzical look on his face, and gave a short, sharp shake of his head, as if he were surprised at his own smile.

Well, it is pretty surprising, she said to herself. *Who'd have guessed it would change his face like that, and make his eyes so...*

Her train of thought was interrupted as she tried to figure out what had changed. It wasn't so much that the smile lightened his expression, it was more that something was missing from his eyes this morning, that shadow that had made her so uneasy before.

Maybe I just haven't caught him early enough until now. Maybe he's just an extreme morning person.

"This really is a beautiful boat," she said.

"Yes," he agreed, not that there was any way to argue the fact. She thought he might offer to show her the rest of it, but he didn't, and she didn't push even though she was curious. Most people were curious about how the "other half" lived, she told herself. There wasn't anything wrong with that.

He flipped the magazine closed. *Aviation Monthly,* she saw on the cover.

"Do you fly?" she asked.

"Yes," he answered, surprising her. She'd somehow expected him to say he was just a wannabe.

Maybe you need to quit making assumptions about him at all, since most of them seem to be wrong, she chided herself.

"So, are you the captain of this boat, too?" she asked, meaning to follow her own advice.

He looked at her steadily for a long, silent moment, as if he knew perfectly well what the others in the marina thought of him. "No," he finally said. "I'm here because the owner's doing me a favor."

"Nice favor," she said, embarrassed all over again now.

"He's a nice guy."

Emma sat and stared into her coffee. She'd never thought of herself as socially inept, in fact she talked to most people fairly easily, but this man was making her feel beyond awkward.

And the fact that she'd just now realized he looked incredibly sexy sitting there in a plain white T-shirt and blue jeans, with his hair tousled, didn't help her one bit.

This is insane, she thought. *I need to sell that boat. Fast.*

"Better get it cleaned up, then," he said easily, startling her into the realization that she'd spoken her thoughts aloud.

"Easy for you to say, at least you know about boats," she said. And was grateful he at least couldn't know that the insane part had been referring to him.

Or rather, her own unexpected reaction to him.

Nine

Harlan was helping her scrub the deck of the *Pretty Lady* when, out of the blue, he startled her by asking a personal—well, personal for him—question.

"So what business did you leave behind to come see what your cousin had left you?"

She was startled, but welcomed the query; after a couple of days of him helping her get the boat in shape to sell, she'd wondered if he ever spoke of anything but vessel maintenance and the weather.

"I run Safe Haven, a nonprofit, long-term shelter for the pets of people in hospitals or nursing homes. We take care of them, and make sure they get to see their people, and vice versa."

Most people smiled at her then, and told her what a wonderful thing she was doing. That was not at all why she did it, it was simply a side benefit. But Harlan stared at her as if she'd said she had started a colony on the moon.

"See their people," he said slowly, as if she'd been speaking a foreign language. "You mean you take in people's dogs and cats?"

"And other pets—rabbits—hamsters, and the occasional ferret. We haven't had any snakes yet, but I suppose that time will come."

"And you do this for free?"

"Not always. People who can pay, do, but we don't turn anyone away. We get a lot of donations, thank goodness. And we have a great vet, Dr. Burke, who looks after us without charging for her services."

He looked amazed, and was slowly starting to shake his head. "How do you survive?"

"We struggle," she admitted. "But it's worth it. I've dreamed of this for a while ever since my grandmother went into the hospital for a long stay and had to give up her spaniel. She loved that dog as much as her grandkids, and it nearly killed her. I think it did contribute to her dying. It's been my dream to keep that from happening to anyone else, so I started Safe Haven."

"That's going a bit far, isn't it?"

"I don't think so. They've done research proving pets can help people get well and stay well, so why shouldn't the opposite also be true?"

He was looking at her as if she were spouting some crackbrain theory about UFOs.

"Imagine," she insisted, "if through no fault of your own but simply by becoming ill and having no one to help, you had to give up your pet. How would you feel?"

He shrugged. Yet again. "I don't know. Never had one."

She gaped at him. "Never? Not even as a kid?"

"No."

"Are you allergic? Was somebody else?"

"No."

"Then why? I mean, I know it would be tough on a boat, but...not even a bird or something?"

His mouth twisted. "You thinking a piratical parrot, or what?"

She had been, sort of, and was embarrassed that he'd caught her in the stereotyping. "I'm sorry. I just can't imagine life without some creature to share it with. They do so much for us, and they're incredible companions to people who are otherwise alone."

"Like the little old lady with twenty cats? No thanks."

"No," Emma said, sharply. "Like the man whose wife of sixty years passes away and leaves him alone for the first time in decades, except for the cat who curls up in his lap at night. Or the kid who's dying of cancer, and the only one that doesn't treat him differently is his dog. Or the—"

"Okay, okay. Sorry," he said, holding up a hand as if to fend her off. "I just always thought of pets as sort of...useless, I guess."

Appalled, Emma stared at him. "You could never say that if you'd ever had one."

He gave her that damned shrug again.

She had never met someone who had that idea in their head. She simply couldn't understand it. Ordinarily she'd assume someone who didn't like animals was cold, hard-hearted or worse, but she knew he wasn't. He wouldn't have helped her the way he had if that was true. But to be fair, he hadn't said he didn't like them, just that he didn't see the point.

So, how could he feel this way? Was it simply that he'd never had a pet? She could easily see where a child who wasn't allowed a pet might decide he didn't want or like them in a sort of self-defense. That had to be it. It was the only thing that made sense to her.

"You've really missed out on a wonderful thing," she said, quietly now. "Everybody needs some unconditional love in their life."

"And you figure you get that from a ferret?"

"A dog was more what I had in mind," she said, refusing to let him bait her. "And that's about the only place you'll get it."

"Don't you ever think your time might be better spent helping people?"

She'd heard this one countless times before. "I happen to think I am helping people by removing this huge worry from their lives. And there are many agencies that help people on a larger scale and better than I could. This is something I can do, so I'm doing it."

He studied her for a moment, and she realized her voice had risen a little at the end.

"I don't judge people for the work they choose," he said softly. "I just wanted to hear what you'd say, since I figured you'd probably been asked that over and over again."

She flushed. "I guess I did get a little...vehement, there." Odd, she thought, she'd done it so often she was usually able to give her reasons less emotionally. But somehow it was very important to her that he get the importance of her work.

"You're passionate about it. That's all anyone should need to know."

She hadn't expected such understanding from him, and if she would have liked for him to agree with her about its importance, she told herself she was being greedy. He was practically a stranger, after all. Although after what they'd been through, he hardly seemed that anymore.

She spent a while longer trying to convince him of what he'd missed out by never sharing his life with man's best companions. He listened, sometimes smiled, sometimes even commented, but she wasn't sure he was convinced.

And it wasn't until much later that she realized that although he had participated in the conversation, he'd managed to go the entire time again without telling her one single thing about himself.

Harlan sat staring at the phone for a long time. *Don't do it,* he told himself. *You're already too involved, don't go any further.*

"One phone call doesn't make me involved," he told himself. Besides, he was curious himself.

He reached for the phone, and three minutes and two connections later was talking to John Draven, Josh Redstone's head of security. The man who had saved his life.

"I'll get back to you," Draven said after Harlan made his request. "Urgent?"

"Not really. I may not do anything with it anyway."

"Tomorrow, then."

Leave it to Draven—or maybe Redstone in general—to consider an answer by tomorrow typical handling of something nonurgent, Harlan thought. And since he'd spent a good portion of his life in places so out of the way that communications that took a week were considered good, waiting a day was nothing.

Especially when he wasn't at all sure he wanted to get the answer anyway.

It was ridiculous that Emma was taking up so much room in his head. He wasn't some kid who couldn't be around an attractive woman without his hormones running amok; he'd left that stage behind him longer ago than he cared to admit. So why was that exactly how he felt? He'd never denied, even to himself, that she was attractive. It had taken him a bit longer to admit she was attracting him.

He wondered now, for the first time, why it had taken him so long to respond to a woman. Was it part of the aftermath of his ordeal, that he was only now coming alive enough to even think about such things? Or was it more, was it Emma herself who had awakened those feelings because…

Because why? Because she had whatever it was his battered spirit and body would respond to?

Getting a little esoteric, there, McClaren, he told himself.

Likely the answer was much simpler. Perhaps it had been working alongside her these past couple of days, watching her intensity and determination. Or maybe it was the way she wasn't afraid of hard work or getting dirty. Or was it something more basic, like the way she moved, the length of her legs, the pert nose?

Now there was nothing esoteric about that, about the simple truth that Emma Purcell turned him on. And considering that until she came along he had feared that wasn't possible anymore, he was almost relieved.

Of course, the fact that he was nowhere near ready to act on that response—despite all the times he'd thought about it—didn't make it any easier, especially when he'd invited her to stay on the *Seahawk*. It was a big boat, but it seemed to be shrinking every minute.

Unlike a certain body part, he grumbled silently.

He heard her footsteps before he saw her. He watched her from the main salon as she came up the dock steps—with much more confidence now, he noted—and stepped down onto the deck. She carried a couple of grocery bags and he frowned, since she'd gone out to pick up some cleaning supplies and urethane to finish the work on the *Pretty Lady*.

"What's all that?" he asked, eyeing the bags as she stepped inside.

He knew he sounded cranky, but somehow her showing up with bags of food only pounded home to him that if he was missing his solitude, it was his own fault for inviting her—practically insisting, in fact—that she stay here after the break-in on the *Pretty Lady*.

If she noticed his tone she didn't react to it. As she began to unload the bags she said only, "I've been eating here so much I figured it was time I kicked in to replenish the fridge."

"You've been cooking," he pointed out, a little less snarly now. "That's more than worth it."

And he meant it; she was a better than good cook.

"I love to cook," she said, gracefully not pointing out that his idea of cooking, which she'd learned the first night after a long day's work sanding and cleaning, was a frozen dinner in the microwave. And he didn't point out that the dinners were gourmet, or that Josh, with his usual flair, had arranged to have them delivered regularly so Harlan didn't have to think about it. Besides, he thought, he had to admit her freshly prepared meals beat even the gourmet frozen stuff.

"And," she added, "you could use some extra weight."

It was the only comment she'd ever made on his appearance, and it almost made him snarlier yet. But the fact that she'd even noticed tamped down that reaction. He wasn't sure exactly why.

What he didn't want to admit was the real reason he was feeling snarly. He'd expected the disruption to his privacy, but not the disruption to his peace of mind. He hadn't expected to be so aware of her presence every moment, to feel a spark ignite every time he looked at her.

He hadn't expected to lie awake at night, picturing the distance between them in his head and calculating just how many steps it was to her stateroom door.

"You do a lot of cooking at home?" he said, more to distract himself from that line of thought than really wanting to carry on a conversation.

"Not as much or as often as I'd like, since there's just me." *No boyfriend?* he wondered. *How did that happen?* "I like it best when some of my family stops by, then I really get to play."

"Stops by?"

She nodded. "We're all within about twenty miles of my folks' house. You like chicken?"

He nodded, but his brow furrowed. "I thought you were angry with your family over Wayne."

"I am." She looked up from setting aside several items, things he guessed she would need to prepare the chicken. "But that doesn't mean I don't love them. Garlic?"

It took him a second. "Yeah. Lots."

She smiled. "A man after my own heart."

I'm not after your heart. Just your body.

   The thought sprang fully formed into his head, and
he found it distractingly odd. It wasn't something he
usually had to remind himself of, it simply was. He
wasn't a man for long-term relationships, never had
been, if for no other reason than he was always about
to move on.

   This was no different, he told himself. Don't forget
you don't have a thing in common with her. All the
things he'd thought before were still true. She lived
within twenty miles of where she'd grown up, and once
he'd left home he'd never been within twenty miles of
anyplace he'd been before. She could barely tolerate
visiting a boat, and he couldn't imagine not living on
one.

   *Hell, she took care of other people's pets, and he'd
never owned so much as a goldfish.*

   It wasn't until that night, after a delicious meal with
enough garlic even for him, when he'd retreated to his
stateroom simply because he was getting too itchy sitting in the same room with her and keeping his distance,
that it struck him. Why was he worried about whether
they had anything in common? It wasn't like he was
planning on marrying the woman, after all. What did it
matter? You didn't have to have things in common if
all you were going to do was have a brief affair.

   Which was all this could be. Because as soon as he
could prove to Josh he was back to normal—or close—
he was out of here, and back to his life. He had places
to go, searching to do, discoveries to make. There was
that wreck off the Carolinas he wanted to dive, and that
promising spot near the Cayman Islands, among others.
And none of those plans included Ms. Emma Purcell.

   Which, he admitted wryly as he watched her put milk,
soda, eggs and butter into the refrigerator and coffee

and oatmeal into the cupboards, *was unlikely to disappoint her very much at all.*

He gave himself a rueful inward smile. Here he'd been doing all this heavy breathing, and she'd never given a sign that she was attracted to him at all.

She thought you were at worst a drug dealer, at the least the person who led her beloved cousin astray, he reminded himself.

But somehow he couldn't get all revved up about that. He might have thought the same thing in her position, if he'd come across somebody who looked like he did just now. He had a mirror, he knew what showed in his face. And she'd gotten over it fairly quickly. More or less. He went to sleep finally, still wondering if all his thinking would lead anywhere. In particular to finding out if his body still functioned in a very important arena.

The phone woke him early. He knew before picking it up that it was Draven; the only person he knew who slept less was St. John, Josh's assistant.

When he hung up a few minutes later, he regretted ever having called. He had his answer, and now he had to make a decision. A difficult one.

Should he tell Emma her beloved and recently departed cousin Wayne had been worse than even he had thought?

Ten

Emma stood in the center of the main cabin of the sailboat, feeling scattered. She didn't know where to start, what to do next. But then, she felt that way in general these days.

She could hear the steady, even sound of Harlan sanding the deck above her head. She'd felt guilty about all the work he was doing, but he'd told her it was good for him. And now the rhythmic cadence was an oddly comforting sound. Just as his presence was oddly comforting. The man was still a mystery to her, yet she was glad he was here. And not just for the help he was giving her.

And that, she realized, was part of the reason for her sense of confusion. She knew virtually nothing about him, was still wary of him, and yet she liked him being around. It had to be because she was still rattled by the break-in. Otherwise it made no sense, and she had been nothing if not logical in her life.

Which, of course, didn't explain why she'd been insane enough to accept his offer of continuing shelter aboard the *Seahawk*. She'd made some big mistakes in her life, but this had to rank up there near the top. The reclusive Harlan McClaren stirred emotions she'd put away long ago. She'd lost her head once over a secretive man, and it had led to disaster. She wasn't about to do it again.

The deck beneath her feet rose suddenly, and her breath caught in her throat. She whirled, half-expecting to see a menacing figure in the hatchway, wondering what had happened to Harlan, why he was still sanding away.

Moments later she realized she'd been hearing the sound of a motor as a boat passed by in the marina, and knew it had to be the wake of that boat that had lifted the *Pretty Lady*.

She sank down on the banquette, barely aware of the shredded condition of the cushion. She shivered, knowing what she'd been afraid of was true. Her eyes brimmed with moisture as a wave of self-condemnation swept over her in the wake of the realization.

She could handle routine things easily, complex things competently, even minor chaos fairly well. But when it came to anything even slightly dangerous, she was a coward.

"Emma, do you want that— What's wrong?"

"Noth-nothing."

"Uh-huh. Try again."

"I'm all right," she said.

"Like hell."

His refusal to let it go sparked something in her. Her

head came up and she glared at him. "I'm not even bleeding."

He drew back slightly, an expression on his face that told her he hadn't missed the reference to his own injury that he had continuously brushed off as nothing.

"Touché," he said softly. He said nothing more for a long, silent moment before guessing, too accurately for her comfort. "You still shaken up by those Neanderthals?"

She didn't look at him. For a moment he did nothing, then he came over and sat down beside her.

"You're safe on the *Seahawk*," he said.

"It's not that."

"What, then?"

She sighed. She needed to talk to somebody, and if he was the last one she would have chosen it was too bad, because he was the only one here.

"I'm such a chicken. All those tools in that room and I never thought to grab one for a weapon."

"Emma—"

"Instead I grab that stupid barometer that splintered like a kite stick."

"You can't be expected to know how to fight like that without any experience, anymore than you could ride a bike without practice. Besides, you slowed him down."

"But didn't stop him. If you hadn't come…"

"You drew blood," he pointed out.

She nearly snorted her own disgust. "Teeth and nails," she said scornfully, unable to meet his eyes.

"You're no coward, Emma."

"Then why am I shaking like a leaf now, when it's long over? Why am I having nightmares? Why do I relive what happened even when I'm awake?"

There was silence for a few moments, then she heard him let out a long, compressed breath.

"Because that's how it happens. Time doesn't matter. Just because it's over in reality doesn't mean it's over in your head. And nothing's worse than not living up to your own expectations."

Her head came up then, and slowly she turned to look at him. His expression was grim, and in that moment she knew he spoke from personal experience.

"How long ago was it for you?" she asked softly.

He tensed, then, with a visible effort, relaxed. "A while."

She hesitated to ask, given his penchant for privacy, but she'd also never seen him this close to opening up. She didn't want to pass up the opportunity.

"What happened?"

It took him a moment, and when he spoke he sounded resigned, but he did speak.

"I was in Nicaragua. Off the beaten path, you might say. Too far off. I should never have gone ashore. I got caught by a jungle warlord named Omar."

"Caught? Like, for trespassing or something?"

"Initially."

"And you...didn't fight?" she asked carefully, wondering if that was what he'd meant.

"Oh, I fought. For all the good it did." He gave her a sideways look. "There were four of them."

"Well, for goodness sake, why didn't you just put on your cape and trounce them all?" she asked, wondering how on earth a man could expect himself to take on four probably armed men. She thought she saw one corner of his mouth quirk, but he said nothing. Finally she prompted him. "What happened?"

For a moment he said nothing, and she sensed how

difficult this was for him, to open up like this. She wondered if he'd ever told anyone before. If he hadn't, the fact that he was telling her, and the reason for it, moved her in a way she'd never felt.

Finally, as if a floodgate had opened, the rest of the story came out.

"He decided if I was American, and was where no American ever dared—or was stupid enough—to go, I must be there under orders."

"Orders?"

"As in CIA."

"Oh, good grief. Why do people always pull out that old nonsense?"

"It's their view of the world, I guess. But he wasn't taking no for an answer."

"What did he expect?"

"He expected me to confess."

"But if you weren't—" She stopped suddenly, her eyes widening. "My God. He tortured you?"

"Let's just say he made sure my stay was as unpleasant as possible."

And just like that she had her answer to his haggard appearance, and it was as far from what she'd imagined as could be. She felt awful about her own silly suspicions.

"Is that what you meant, about not living up to your own expectations? You confessed? My God, Harlan, POWs have been forced under torture to do the same, and nobody blames them. No one can be expected to hold out against—"

"I didn't confess," he said, cutting her off.

"Then what on earth are you feeling guilty about?"

"Because I wouldn't confess, Omar executed an innocent man."

Her eyes widened again. It sounded so surreal to her, so foreign to her, that she wondered for a moment if this wasn't some wild tale concocted to impress her, or for some other nefarious reason. But one look in his haunted eyes told her every word was painfully true. And in today's world, she should know better than to believe anyplace was safe.

"Who?" she asked, her voice barely above a whisper.

"My guide, Miguel. He was a good man, with a wife and three kids."

"The poor woman. And children."

"They'll want for nothing," he said determinedly, and she wondered if he sent them money, if that was why he had to bum a place to live off his rich friend. That put a whole new light on it, and once more she was ashamed of her assumptions.

"How did you get out?"

"That nice guy who owns the *Seahawk* sent someone after me. Luckily before Omar started killing the rest of my crew, one by one. And before he did any permanently incapacitating damage to me."

She shivered, suddenly feeling very isolated in her safe little world. "I'm sorry," she said, meaning it.

"Me, too. I hear that shot every night. He never even threatened to do it, just did it."

"You can't expect logic from a madman." She gave him a sideways look. "Speaking of madmen and what they do, what were you doing in Nicaragua in the first place?"

He had the grace to give her a rueful smile, not denying the "madman" tag. "I was searching for something."

"Must have been an important something."

''Only if you believe in legends,'' he said cryptically.

Already she knew better than to pursue when he began to dodge. ''Is that why you're here? To…recuperate?''

He nodded. ''And put it behind me.''

''Is it working?''

He shrugged, that maddening nonanswer. But this time she at least got some words to go with it. ''They say I should be physically fine soon. Nobody could tell me when, or if, the nightmares would stop.''

He lapsed into silence, and for a long moment she just sat there, absorbing what he'd said. In the end, there was only one more thing she wanted to ask, although it took her even longer to get it out. Finally the words came.

''Why did you tell me?''

He looked at her straight on this time, and she saw the shadows of what he'd been through in his eyes. ''Because I've been living where you've been the past couple of days. It's not a good place, Emma. Don't take up residence.''

It was an answer, but not the one she'd wanted.

She'd wanted to know why he'd told *her*.

She was only here aboard the *Seahawk,* Harlan told himself the next morning, because of the burglary of the *Pretty Lady.* Of course she didn't want to go back and stay on the boat she hadn't wanted in the first place.

But that didn't help him much in the night, when his body was all too aware of her, sleeping warm and soft down the hall. When his mind came up with all kinds of reasons to go to her, ranging from an altruistic making sure she wasn't afraid, to a more realistic need to make sure his body still worked.

He only wished he was more certain that's all it was. He didn't want to feel anything more than a physical urge. Well, maybe friendship, he could stand that. But nothing more. Especially with a woman like Emma. She was just another one who wouldn't understand his passions. He'd already lost a wife, a fiancé, and his belief in enduring love to his devotion to what he loved most in life.

He clung still to the words of the psychologist Josh had insisted he see after he'd been rescued and brought home. She had told him everything might feel more profound, more intense for a while. That was all this was, he assured himself. Emma was really no different, there was nothing special about her that spoke to something deep inside him.

He had himself almost completely convinced of that by morning. He got up and dressed quickly, in the best mood he'd been in for days, now that he had it worked out. It was, after all, simply something he had to get through, just like the healing of his body.

He caught himself humming as he stepped out of his stateroom. But the sound caught in his throat as he spotted Emma, wrapped only in a towel as she dodged quickly down the hall from the head to the next door down, her stateroom.

Good Lord, her legs went on forever, he thought almost reverently. And obviously the upper curves were all real and all hers; you couldn't fake that kind of thing in a towel.

His fledgling confidence shattered, he nearly retreated to his room to hide.

You're going to want to hide from the world, the shrink had said. *Don't. That's imperative. And I promise you it will get easier.*

"Easy for you to say," he muttered as he made himself walk past the door that separated him from temptation and go up to the main salon.

Nothing in the galley appealed to him, so he poured a mug of coffee and headed up to the bridge. He hadn't fired up the engines since Emma had come aboard, so he needed to do that. He checked gauges, set switches, then hit the ignition. She fired up sweetly, as always, and he could feel in the deck beneath his feet the barely perceptible humming of a ship come alive.

Harlan ran through a series of diagnostic tests. He'd never had a boat as sophisticated as the *Seahawk,* but he did his best, knowing that normally Josh would have a minimum crew of three or four on board full-time, just for maintenance. The demands of Redstone limited Josh to just a few trips up here a year, and when he did come up, he wanted the boat ready to go.

Everything appeared to be running smoothly. Like his airplanes, the boats Josh built were pure quality and efficiency, designed for people who chose those things over gloss and flash. And while that full-time crew might make things easier, the *Seahawk* was designed so that one person could handle her. Josh knew what it was like to want to be alone, Harlan thought.

He studied the bank of dials and readouts on the wall behind the helm. There was one gauge on a compressor for the air-conditioning, rarely used here in the Northwest but necessary in the Tropics, that wasn't reading as it should be; he'd have to check it out and see if it was really the compressor or a faulty gauge. He hoped it was—

The sound of her footsteps outside the door to the bridge was the only warning he had. He made himself continue to study the control panel even after she came in.

"I heard the motor start," she said after a moment.

He glanced at her then, registered her cautious expression. "Thinking I was about to cast off? With you unwillingly aboard, no doubt?"

He saw by the faint flush that colored her cheeks that he'd hit the target dead center.

"Suspicious, aren't you?" He lifted an eyebrow at her. "Not that the idea doesn't have a certain appeal."

Her color deepened, and he sternly told himself she was merely embarrassed, not agreeing with him.

"I guess I am," she admitted. "I'm still edgy about being on a boat. Although I have to say, I would never have thought I could relax as much as I have on this one."

"She's a good boat for that. Solid."

"Is it working for you?" she asked, startling him with the quick change of subject.

"Maybe," he allowed, not sure if what was happening to him was exactly what Josh had in mind. Then again, Josh was a big believer in happy ever after. For everyone but himself, anyway.

His breath caught, and for a moment he was unable to swallow as he realized what he'd just done. That he had linked what was happening to him, his ever more tangled feelings about Emma Purcell, with Josh Redstone's belief in happy endings. Romantic happy endings. What idiotic corner of his subconscious had come up with that?

"Harlan?"

He only realized how he must be gaping at her when she gave him that puzzled look. "What did you want? Just to make sure I wasn't kidnapping you?"

She frowned, and he knew his effort at diversion had come out sharply. So be it, he thought. The best defense and all.

"Something to do with that?" he asked, indicating the piece of paper she held in one hand.

"Oh. Oh, yes. I wanted to show it to you."

"What is it?"

"It's…" She faltered, then began again. "Perhaps I should back up a little. Since you're the only recent friend of Wayne's that I know, I thought maybe you might have an idea about this."

"What is it?" he repeated, wary now.

"It's a letter from him. I got it three days after he died."

He saw the tiny shiver in the moment before she suppressed it. "Must have been…spooky."

"Very. He mailed it the day before, from here."

She held it out to him. He didn't want to take it. Didn't even want to make contact, as if simply touching it could somehow suck him more deeply into this confusing maelstrom he was already fighting.

But she just stood there, waiting, looking at him with those eyes. And almost against his volition, he was reaching for the envelope she held.

"You sure you want me to read this?"

She nodded. "You were closest to him at the end. Maybe it will make more sense to you."

He doubted that. If Wayne's lack of sobriety in those last days was anything to go by, he wasn't surprised that whatever he'd written here made no sense. Reluctantly, he reached into the envelope and pulled out the letter, a page that appeared worn by much unfolding and refolding.

His brows furrowed. It was on *Seahawk* stationery,

the rich, pale gray vellum with the outline of the boat
and her name in a deep red script, the Redstone colors.
He wondered when Wayne had snagged the paper. The
writing was a clumsy, shaky scrawl except, he noticed
immediately, at the very end, where the last line was
printed carefully, and with some force, he noted, the
pen having dug into the thick paper hard enough to
leave grooves on the other side.

His gaze naturally skipped to the carefully printed
line. "Look to the *Pretty Lady* for the answer. She holds
her secrets deep, but they're there." Curious now, he
went up to the top and read from the beginning. Or tried
to; the writing was nearly illegible in several places.

From what he could tell, the rambling letter consisted
mostly of Wayne's usual diatribe; nothing was ever his
fault, everyone hated him through no fault of his own
and someday he was going to be rich enough to tell the
world and his family to go to hell. Except for Emma,
of course. He made that quite clear, and Harlan had to
admit that this part at least rang true; Wayne really had
loved his cousin.

And why not? What's not to love?

He winced. That damned subconscious of his not
only had too much time on its hands, it was starting to
become vocal.

"I've heard most of the tirade before," he told her
bluntly. "The last line is the only thing that's different."

If she was insulted by his words, she didn't show it.
"That's what I mean," she said. "That last part."

"What do you think it means?" he asked.

"The only thing I can think of is that it means Wayne
had some kind of feeling he might…be in trouble."

"You mean a premonition?"

She nodded, her eyes troubled. "That he might die."

Well, that would have been a no-brainer, Harlan thought. If anything, Wayne might have had a booze or drug-induced hallucination. Or maybe the self-knowledge that his abuses would someday be fatal.

But he did have to admit it bothered him, and had all along, that it had been the rundown, at best ordinary-looking *Pretty Lady* that had been broken into. Especially since the clearly much richer prize of the *Seahawk* was close by. It made the likelihood that that burglary had been random much slimmer. Which would put Emma in possible danger if she returned to the *Pretty Lady.*

Which made it impossible for him to suggest she do so and leave him—and his asinine subconscious—in peace.

Eleven

He thought she was crazy, Emma concluded. She'd seen it in his eyes when she'd suggested Wayne had known something was going to happen to him. So she'd excused herself hastily and retreated to the main salon. She should never have broached that without her morning coffee first.

She supposed she couldn't blame him. They didn't seem to see eye to eye on some pretty basic things. But this seemed a bit more serious than him thinking she was nuts for being afraid of boats, and her thinking he was nuts for how he felt about pets.

She could understand why he didn't think much of Wayne. He'd never known the sweet, charming, lively boy he'd been, only the bitter, reckless man he'd apparently become. It hurt her to admit it, but Harlan had no reason to lie to her. She would still never admit that his judgmental parents hadn't helped him along the wrong path with their impossible demands and harsh punishments, but she was having trouble denying he'd become just what they'd predicted.

She was halfway through her first cup of coffee—with the rich, luscious blend served aboard the *Seahawk,* she could rarely resist a second one—when the engines shut down. Then, after a few minutes, they started again. Then shut down and started once more, apparently while he worked on something. They shut down again. The time ticked by as she waited, almost holding her breath, for Harlan to appear in the doorway.

When, after several minutes, he didn't come, she figured he must be doing some other work on the engines, or up on the…bridge? Was that what it was called, even on a private boat? Yacht? Whatever this was, she finished wryly. Floating mansion, most likely.

That brought to mind her own—how odd to be thinking that about a boat!—less glamorous vessel. She should be over there working, not sitting here sipping expensive coffee that wasn't hers.

She rinsed out her coffee mug and headed out and over to the *Pretty Lady,* wondering as she went about something that had been bothering her ever since he'd told her about his disastrous time in the jungle.

What on earth had he been doing in a place where someone like his captor could grab him? The average person hardly woke up one morning and decided to head off to the Nicaraguan jungle. And ''searching for something'' was hardly a satisfying or informative answer.

She was just too nosy, she thought, turning on herself. It was really none of her business. But at the same time, she couldn't think of one other person she'd spent this much time with and ended up knowing so little about.

She kept sanding on the bow deck, already starting to feel the burn of muscles in her arms and shoulders, and more potently, the pressure on her knees as she worked. It wasn't enough to keep her from ruefully admitting that the lack of knowledge about Harlan wouldn't matter so much if she wasn't so attracted to him.

She glanced over at the *Seahawk,* but saw no sign of him, although she'd heard the engines fire up and now they were running steadily, and had been for the last half hour or so. He must be working on them again today.

She decided it was a good thing to have taken this time away from him. They'd been in close quarters working together on the *Pretty Lady,* and spending nights aboard the *Seahawk,* which had somehow seemed much bigger when she'd first stepped aboard. After the first couple of nights, after she'd caught up on her sleep, she'd found herself awakening in the middle of the night and spending too long thinking about how he was just down the hall.

It simply wasn't like her to fall for somebody like him. Not that she was certain what she meant by ''like him.'' She frowned, seeing the inkling of a flaw in her logic. She knew he could and would work hard. That he would do it for a stranger, just to help. She doubted it was just the Wayne connection; he'd done far more already than that slight acquaintance would warrant.

He'd given no indication he expected anything in return. Nor had he put any pressure on her in a sexual way.

But he'd looked, she thought, her heart speeding up at the thought, as it had every time she remembered glimpsing him at the end of the hall when she'd darted out of the shower and back into the stateroom. Yes, he'd looked, and if his expression had been anything to judge by, he hadn't minded what he'd seen. She might be less experienced than some of her friends, but she recognized heat when she saw it.

And now that she had acknowledged that, what next?

Nothing, she answered herself firmly. Acknowledging an attraction didn't mean you had to do anything about it. Although, if she was right and the feeling was mutual…

Stop it. You came here to handle Wayne's bequest, nothing more.

She attacked the deck with new vigor.

It still didn't help.

She'd thought she'd be so exhausted after the day of hard work that she would sleep through the night. She didn't. At 3:00 a.m. she was wide awake. She tried to blame it on the amount of caffeinated soda she'd consumed while working, but she knew that wasn't it.

Wearily, still feeling the effects of her day's efforts, she got up, pulled on some sweats and a T-shirt, and headed up to the galley, wondering if she could find something soothing like hot chocolate. Even as she thought it, she smiled inwardly; she doubted there was much that the *Seahawk* didn't have in its larders. Harlan had told her to get whatever she wanted, so she felt odd but not guilty as she found what she was looking for in the cabinet next to the refrigerator.

Thanks to a microwave that made hers look like an antique, she had the steaming drink in her hands in seconds.

She'd noticed on her way up here that there was a lot of light coming in from outside. It had been overcast last night, but tonight was clear again, and when she stepped outside to look, she found a world awash in the silver of moonlight. It was both beautiful and eerie.

She let the door close behind her and walked farther out on the deck, looking up at the full, white orb and the watery trail it left across water that was incredibly smooth tonight. That comforted her. This water, she thought, she could live with. And the transition that thought indicated still amazed her. She would never have imagined she could—

"It's beautiful, isn't it?"

His voice came from behind her and her breath caught. She found herself pressing a hand to her chest in a motion she ruefully thought looked like some old-time melodrama queen. Or her mother. She barely managed not to whirl around and betray her silliness to him. Instead she glanced back over her shoulder, as casually as she could.

"Yes," she finally got out, although belatedly. "It is."

"Glassy tonight."

He stepped up close behind her, and it took her a moment to realize he was talking about the water. "Yes," she repeated, sounding inane to her own ears.

"Dangerous, though."

An undertone had come into his voice, one that made her suddenly itchy. She wondered what fearsome thing might be lurking under that glassy surface, or if he just meant this quiet was the precursor to something more unsettled. "What do you mean?"

"All this moonlight. Makes people think of things to do in it."

And suddenly, without moving an inch, he was too close. Much too close. She could feel the light, feathery brush of his breath on the back of her neck. Could feel the heat of him radiating toward her, seeming to envelop her. Her heart leaped into overdrive, and she sucked in a deep breath just to be sure she could breathe at all.

"Moonlight," he said, his voice a low rumble in her ear, "makes things that are hard to resist in the day impossible to resist."

She felt him shift slightly, and before she was aware of what he was doing she felt his lips on the nape of her neck. Lightly, barely touching, a whisper of warmth in a sensitive spot she'd never known she had. It didn't seem possible that such a slight touch could send warmth rippling through her, but it did.

And then she felt a wet, slick heat as his tongue flicked over her skin. What had been a pleasant warmth erupted into flame. And perversely, a shiver rippled through her, as if she were chilled instead of suddenly...hot.

As that last word formed in her mind a new kind of heat flooded her, a tension-building combination of embarrassment and anticipation. And then his mouth moved, up the side of her throat to her ear. The soft, warm rush of his breath there made her shiver yet again. And then his tongue touched her again, circling her ear, making her feel hot and cold at the same time. And this time a shudder went through her that she was helpless to stop.

She said his name, and it came out like a plea. A plea for what, she wasn't sure. Logic said "stop," but her body had other ideas, and was clamoring "more" until she could barely stand it.

"I knew you'd be sweet," he whispered, his voice so low it was almost broken. "But I never knew anything could be that sweet."

This was crazy, Emma thought. She couldn't believe she was doing this. Not with this man she barely knew. It was totally unlike her. It had to stop, and she turned around to face him and tell him so. But as she turned, his arms came up and surrounded her in an embrace that felt all the more exciting for the warm, safe feeling it gave her. A feeling which was as absurd as the fact that she was simply standing here, letting him hold her far too closely.

Letting him? a little voice in the back of her mind taunted.

Okay, truth be known, she wasn't just letting him. She was liking it. A lot.

This time she saw him move, knew what was coming. But as if he'd still been behind her and she had no clue she simply stood still. Waiting. His finger came up under her chin, and he tilted her head back.

"Emma," he whispered, and she thought that in his voice gone husky, her plain, boring name was the most beautiful thing she'd ever heard.

What was he waiting for? she wondered absently as he stared down into her eyes. She was certain he was going to kiss her. She was also certain she wanted him to, more than she wanted to keep breathing. When he still didn't move, she realized in some yet-unfogged part of her brain that he was waiting for some sign from her.

She parted her lips to speak, even knowing words were beyond her just now. She swallowed tightly, tried again, failed again. But it didn't matter, because Harlan seemed to understand her silent response. Slowly he lowered his head. The last remnant of her common sense told her, given what the merest touch of his lips and tongue had done to her, that she'd best be ready for a serious conflagration.

It was her last coherent thought. The moment his lips met hers, she went up in flames, not even aware of how right she'd been. And not caring. She didn't care about anything except the feel of his mouth on hers, and the fire that was racing along what felt like every nerve in her body.

She clutched at his arms, her fingers digging in as she held on to the only thing that seemed capable of keeping her upright in her suddenly hot, liquid world. Her head spun until she felt like she used to feel being on water; weak, shaky and out of control.

And then his hand moved, slowly, caressingly, until his fingers curled to cup her breast through her T-shirt. Her flesh molded itself to his hand, fitting perfectly, making her ache for more, much more.

When he at last broke the kiss she nearly cried out at the loss of that wonderful heat. But an instant later, as a horn from an incoming ferryboat echoed across the water, reality crashed in on her. Muscles that had been warmed to softness seconds ago stiffened abruptly.

Harlan seemed to sense it, and drew back slightly. She looked up at him.

"Moonlight is potent," he said softly. "And depending on your point of view, sometimes toxic."

He let her go then, and she felt relieved when he turned and disappeared into the *Seahawk*. But her relief vanished when she realized that what she felt more than anything else was a sense of loss.

And the urge to call him back.

Twelve

Moonlight didn't just make him crazy, it made him stupid. That was the only explanation for what he'd done.

Well, that and the fact that he was about to jump out of his skin just being around her. And he was tired of feeling like he was teetering on the edge every night, waffling between getting as far away as possible and running to her as fast as he could.

And if you'd known what kind of reception you'd get?

He sighed at his own thought, knowing the answer to the question. If he'd known she'd go up in flames at the merest touch, he'd have been climbing into her bunk a long time ago. And now that he knew, how the hell was he going to keep from doing just that?

Idiot, he told himself. *You're lying here in agony, watching that same moonlight stream in through the porthole, thinking of how she looked, how she re-*

sponded. And you've no one to blame but yourself. I hope you're happy now, McClaren.

He'd tried to calm his revved up body with a cold shower, but without much luck. He dozed now and then, but never missed an hour on the clock. Fortunately, the sun rose early this time of year, so at five he gave up and rose to get started on his day. Such as it would be. He'd ordered the new gauge, but he'd have to find something else to do until it got here.

He realized with more than a little passing surprise that he was feeling better. Not nearly as good as new, but most definitely better than he'd been when he'd come here. He had more energy, tired less easily, and for the first time he allowed himself to hope the end might be in sight.

To his surprise, Emma was apparently already up, and judging from the gorgeous smell, had coffee on. If it wasn't for that, and his need for a caffeine infusion, he would have retreated and found something to do at the other end of the boat. He really didn't want to face her, coward that he was. But he needed that coffee.

The moment he saw her face, and she gave him that shy, hesitant smile, he knew it was going to be as bad as he'd feared. He didn't know what to say to her. Say nothing to her? Apologize for moonlight madness? Act like it hadn't happened at all?

He liked that last alternative. But he somehow doubted she was going to let him get away with that one. He could practically see words he didn't want to hear hovering in her mind. She moved toward him, as if she expected him to pick up where he'd left off last night.

So instead, he spoke first. ''You going back to work on that white elephant your beloved Wayne left you?''

She blinked and drew back slightly, and only then did he realize how sharp his words had sounded. But he was happier with her backing off a little, felt safer somehow.

"You said it was all he had, so how can I belittle it?"

"Guess I'm just thinking that if he cared so much, he would have done better." He knew he sounded snarly, but it was rising in him and he couldn't seem to hold it back.

"I'm sure he tried—"

"Damn, Emma, when are you going to stop making excuses for him?" His vehemence startled her, but he'd known it was coming.

"He was—"

"A fantasy! Your image of him was built on the kid you knew, and that kid ceased to exist long ago."

"You didn't know him then," she said, a desperate sort of pain echoing in her voice. One part of him wanted to back off, to ease that pain, but another, angry part of him wanted to tear the blinders from her eyes and make her face the truth.

"No. I only know what he was at the end. He was a drunk and a druggie. And it wasn't new, he'd been at it for years. It was a miracle he didn't die long ago, and a bigger one that he didn't take some innocent person out with him!"

Her head lowered, and he saw her blink rapidly several times.

Damn it, I wanted her to get angry, not hurt.

He'd expected her, with her blind loyalty to her dead cousin, to get furious with his cold, scathing assessment. He'd expected her to turn on him. And to walk away.

The realization hit him low and hard. *He'd wanted her to walk away.*

He'd never played this kind of game before, trying to drive a woman away. So why now? Why was it so important that he drive Emma away, so important that his gut had taken over and done it before he even realized what was happening?

That gut shouted the answer at him now. *She's getting too close,* it chanted in his head, over and over and over.

But he knew that was the simple answer. The obvious one. The real one was beneath the surface, and he was in no way ready to look at it.

She lifted her head and looked at him, and he could see the moisture brimming in her eyes. That he'd done that to her made him feel slightly queasy.

"I didn't mean to throw that at you like that," he said contritely, although the truth was that it was exactly what he'd meant to do. What he hadn't planned was her reaction.

"Sometimes the truth hurts." Her voice was sad, and weary, as if she'd fought against believing this for a long time. As he supposed she had.

"Emma—"

She held up a hand to stop him. "It's all right. I know it's true. Wayne was much more screwed up than I realized."

She gave him a sideways look that matched her unhappy tone. And Harlan's chest tightened. Even though it was true, he regretted his outburst now. She'd obviously undergone a sea change about her late cousin, and to his surprise, Harlan didn't like it much.

"I just didn't want to admit it. That the boy I loved so much could have gotten so...lost. And I *couldn't* admit, after all this time of fighting them over it, that my family was right all along.''

He shouldn't have pushed her to this, he thought. The knowledge was too painful. He should have protected her from it, not shoved it in her face.

Protected her?

The words echoed in his head, shaking him. He couldn't remember the last time he'd ever wanted to protect anyone. Usually he figured people pretty much got what they deserved. Even himself; he'd known what he was risking when he trekked into that backwater jungle, and when he'd been captured it had been the luck of the draw. He'd gotten out of worse places unscathed, so he figured his number had just come up that time. It hadn't helped him get over it, but it was one less thing to haunt him.

So why wasn't he figuring Emma had this coming, that she needed the scales pulled from her eyes and if the process hurt, so be it? Why was he sitting here wishing, if nothing else, that he hadn't been the one to do it?

''I must seem like a fool to you,'' she began, but stopped when he shook his head.

''You're loyal,'' he said. ''There's a lot to be said for that.''

''There's a fine line between loyalty and blindness,'' she suggested, quoting his own words back at him.

''That, too,'' he admitted. ''But as long as you see the light eventually…''

She sighed. ''I suppose. But I don't like it.''

''Nobody said you have to like it. It's ignorance that's bliss.''

''I wasn't ignorant. I was in denial. Somewhere in my heart I knew, I just didn't want to believe.''

"It's hard to be let down by someone you trusted."

"I hate it," she muttered, "when people turn out not to be who I think they are."

Oops.

Now there's a problem, he thought. What if she discovers the truth about you? Will she be glad about who you really are, or just angry that you didn't tell her?

"I think I'll go get started. I need to work."

He opened his mouth to say he'd be over to help, but nothing came out. He watched her leave in silence, knew she was still wrestling with the realization she had never wanted to have.

And so was he. And the knowledge that had just descended on him shook him to the core.

He didn't want her to find out about him. That part he understood. What had him so rattled, was that the reason why had just struck him.

He didn't want her to find out about him yet, because he didn't want it to affect how she felt about him. Not that he was sure about how she did feel. Or how he wanted her to feel. He just knew he wanted to know how she felt before all that got in the way.

And if there was a reason for that, it was buried deep, much deeper than he was ready to dig right now.

She hadn't needed Harlan's outburst to make her see. Emma meant what she'd told him. On some level, she'd spent a little too long rationalizing, a little too much effort finding excuses, a little too much energy denying what was right in front of her.

And no matter what Harlan had said, she couldn't help feeling like Wayne had made a fool of her. At the least she felt stupid for not having seen the truth long ago. Except that maybe he hadn't been this bad when she'd last seen him.

Or was that just making excuses again?

She gave a weary sigh and went back to the seemingly endless sanding. She didn't know anymore. The only thing she knew for sure was that her heart was heavy and her mind weary of the thoughts whirling around in her head.

"How could you let it happen like that, Wayne?" she asked of no one. There was no fierceness in the words, only sadness.

She made herself focus on what she was doing, even though the job was fairly mindless. She wondered why on earth anyone would buy anything that required this amount of work. It was like the Golden Gate bridge, she thought. You sanded and sweated and painted from one end to the other, and by then it was time to go back to the beginning and start over.

"You could rent a sander."

She stopped, sat back on her heels and looked at Harlan as he stood on the dock. She'd half expected him not to come over today. But now that he had, now that he was right in front of her, she had to confess in her mind at least, that one of the reasons she was so upset was that she'd had no chance to bring up what had happened between them last night. And while she might have been blind when it came to her cousin, she wasn't stupid, and it didn't take much for her to guess that that was exactly what Harlan had intended. Which it seemed to her meant only one thing; he regretted it.

What did you expect? she asked as she watched him come aboard. *You're hardly the irresistible type, especially needing a haircut and carrying those extra twenty pounds.*

"Now you tell me about a sander," she said. Then, rather glumly, "But I probably couldn't afford it anyway."

He crouched beside her. "Dogs eating up all your money?"

She stiffened. "Just because you've led a life deprived of the best companionship a human being can have gives you no right to criticize someone who hasn't. And would never want to."

He winced. "Okay, okay, lousy wisecrack. It was a joke, though. Really, I have nothing against dogs. I just don't know much about them."

He sounded sincere enough, so she let her ire fade away. She studied him for a moment. "I could fix that," she said.

Something must have shown in her eyes, because he looked at her warily. "I'm not sure I like whatever you have in mind."

"You couldn't help but like what I have in mind," she told him, an image of him with a gamboling, sweet-natured puppy forming in her mind with such clarity it startled her.

She heard him make an odd, tight little sound, as if his breath had caught in his throat. It was a sound that made what she'd said play back in her head, and when it did her own breath caught. She opened her mouth to explain what she'd meant, but decided she would only make things worse and shut it again. Tightly.

She turned back to her job, and didn't look up when he joined her in the sanding.

"Emma?" he said after several minutes of silence.

"Yes?" It came out somewhere between stiff and prim.

"Lighten up."

She didn't know whether to be hurt or angry. But when she realized she was sitting here analyzing how she should respond to the simple request, she couldn't help herself. She started to laugh.

"Sometimes," she said ruefully, "I take myself and my work too seriously."

"Maybe because there are a lot of people who don't take your work seriously enough," he said, surprising her.

"There are those," she agreed, not pointing out the obvious, that he was one of them.

"I did a little reading online. Those studies you talked about. Specifically the one from the Center for Disease Control."

Startled now, she stared at him. "You did?"

He nodded. "I had no idea the effects could be so physical. Lowering blood pressure, even cholesterol, all that."

"Serious stuff," she said, pleased more than she would ever have imagined that he had bothered. "And even just a visit with a pet helps. Full-time companionship gives even more, long-term benefits." She gave him a sideways look. "That's why you could use a dog."

"Not much room on a boat. And I wouldn't want an ankle biter."

"Oh, no, you're a big dog man, I'm sure. But there are dogs who are very adaptable, as long as they get enough exercise. Besides, you won't be on this boat forever, will you? I mean, after you…recuperate?"

She really hadn't meant to pry, but as soon as the words left her mouth she realized she was anxious to hear his answer. How long was he going to be here? And where would he go when he finally left?

"I don't know," he said lazily, "I could get used to living like this."

Having had a taste of the *Seahawk*'s luxury, she could understand that. But she still couldn't quite get used to the idea of living off someone else. Even if he did work on the boat in return.

But she still didn't have an answer to her question. And she had no way of getting one without making it obvious she wanted to know for personal, not canine reasons. She sighed inwardly. And then, unexpectedly, he answered her.

"I don't know what I'm going to do, where I'm going to go. I'll have to start thinking about it soon, but…"

She thought of what he'd been through, and nodded. "Not something you want to rush."

They worked quietly together for a while longer, then he said, "I could rent that sander for you."

And charge it to your rich friend? she wondered. "No thanks," she said.

But as the next couple of days went by, and he worked alongside her as if he had some personal investment in the *Pretty Lady,* she began to question her assessment of him yet again. After all, her judgment about men was bad—Wayne had proved that with painful finality—so why couldn't it work both ways, good and bad? Maybe she was mistaken about Harlan as well.

Now that's some rationalization, she told herself. *More likely you just don't want to admit you're so attracted to a bum.*

Thirteen

Although it wasn't really hot—it only rarely ever got to even eighty degrees here on the water—you couldn't tell it by the temperature in the engine room. Harlan had pulled off his shirt half an hour ago and was wishing he'd put on swimming trunks to come down here and redo the wiring for the new gauge that had arrived this morning.

Admit it, he told himself. *It's the damn close quarters as much as anything.*

He knew it was the truth. While the *Seahawk*'s engine room wasn't small for a boat this size, it was too small for Harlan. It was just about the size of the basement cell they'd kept him in, and what should have been the first hour of work in here had taken him three, simply because he kept having to go topside just to show himself he could, that he wasn't chained to this wall.

He'd spent days like that, trying to do routine main-

tenance on the engines. Each time he managed to stay
down longer, until he'd at last gotten nearly forty-five
minutes of uninterrupted work done, reading gauges,
checking for leaks and determining the problem he'd
noted on the bridge was likely the gauge, not the ma-
chinery. And today he'd managed to replace the gauge
in one nearly unbroken session. He was feeling pretty
pleased with himself when he shut down and headed up
and out of the small room for the last time.

At least he was until he realized Emma was waiting
on the deck.

He froze in his tracks. More than anything he wanted
to run, to dodge out of sight, even if it meant going
back into the engine room. But he couldn't seem to
move. At all.

He only had time to notice she must have been working hard, her hair and skin damp with perspiration, before he saw it all register. Saw her eyes as she looked
at him, at his bare torso, saw them widen as she took
in the scars, the marks, the evidence of the damage done
to his body. The burns across his belly, the knife cuts
on his chest, the vicious claw marks where Omar had
loosed his pet leopard on him. It was like one of his
nightmares come to life.

"Seen enough?" His voice came out sharply as she
continued to stare.

Her eyes finally rose to his face. "He did all that to
you? This Omar?"

"He was very creative."

She grimaced. "I hope he's very dead."

Startled at the vehemence in her tone, Harlan drew
back slightly. He hadn't expected that reaction, let alone
her vehemence. He'd expected pity, not anger.

"I don't know," he said finally. "If I'd had my

druthers I'd have made certain before I left, but it wasn't my decision. Besides, he was already at war with most of his neighbors. Chances are one of them caught up with him by now.''

Her gaze flickered down his body again. He stood there, hating it, until the muscles of his belly began to tighten involuntarily under her steady regard. He once again nearly broke and ran. But then she spoke.

''I admire your strength,'' she said softly.

''Strength?'' He nearly snorted. It had taken him weeks of steadily increasing, painful exercise to get even to this point. When he'd first gotten here, he'd been barely able to walk the length of the dock without resting.

But she nodded. ''The kind it takes to merely survive something like that. Those scars are like badges, that you came through something that would have destroyed most, mentally if not physically.''

He almost told her how close it had come to destroying him. How, by the time Draven had arrived, Harlan had thought of telling him to leave him there, because he was going to die one way or another anyway. But Draven had orders from Josh, so anything Harlan had said would have been ignored anyway. He didn't know Draven's history with Josh Redstone, but he knew the man would literally march into hell if Josh asked him to.

But then, he wasn't sure he wouldn't, too, if Josh asked. The man inspired loyalty like no one Harlan had ever known.

''I know I would never make it through something like that,'' she said.

''Don't sell yourself short,'' he said. ''Most women are tougher than men.''

She shook her head. "Not me. I cry at sappy commercials."

"Not necessarily related," he said. "My dad used to get weepy at Disney movies, and he was the toughest guy I ever knew. Well, second toughest," he amended.

"First being…the man who rescued you?"

She was quick, but then he already knew that. He nodded. "Now, if you don't mind, I've been on display long enough." He couldn't believe he'd stood here this long.

"I'm sorry," she said. "I didn't mean to stare, but…"

"Yeah, I know. It's pretty pitiful."

Her gaze shot to his face and their eyes locked. "Seeing you like this makes me feel many things," she said softly. "But pity is *not* one of them."

She turned then, and walked away without saying another word. She'd been out of sight for a long moment before he could breathe normally again.

He wasn't sure he believed her, that she felt no pity for him. If he believed that, then he had to wonder what else she'd meant, what she did feel. *Seeing you like this makes me feel many things….* What *had* she meant?

He knew what he wanted her to mean. He wanted her to mean looking at him made her feel like he did when he looked at her. He didn't want to be alone in this, didn't want to be the only one feeling this insanity rising inside.

He headed below to take a shower, hoping it would still his whirling thoughts. But as he peeled off his jeans he caught sight of himself in the mirror. And unlike every other time, this time he looked.

Those scars are like badges…

He'd never thought of them like that, mainly because

he tried never to think of them at all. Seeing them reminded him of what a weakling he'd been, thinking only of his own pain while Miguel was marched into the jungle and coldly murdered.

There had been many women who had looked at this body and called it sexy. But that was before. He'd thought of trying to contact one of them to see just how much the lines of twisted flesh and puckered scars repulsed them. But when he thought of talking to them now, those women he'd had the shallowest of relationships with, it just wasn't worth the effort.

Emma, on the other hand…

He spun on his heel and dove into the shower as if the room had caught fire.

It took her several minutes alone in her stateroom to calm her jittery nerves, and longer still for her pulse to slow. This was ridiculous. She lived in California, for crying out loud. She'd seen a million guys without shirts on. She'd seen maybe thousands in bathing suits alone. And some of those suits had been next to nonexistent. She'd admired some, barely noticed others and winced at the ones displaying more than they should in one way or another. But none of them had ever stopped her breath the way Harlan had.

To be honest, the first thing that had grabbed her attention had been the scars.

…he made sure my stay was as unpleasant as possible.

Unpleasant. What a mild, throwaway word for what had been done to him. She couldn't begin to imagine the horror and pain he'd endured.

Just because it's over in reality doesn't mean it's over in your head.

Still endured, she amended as his words came back to her. Her nightmares had been bad enough; his must be utterly horrific.

And now that she'd seen those scars, she felt another pang of guilt that she'd ever thought he should be moving on, off the charity of his friend. Anyone who had been through that should get to spend the rest of his life at peace, she thought. And if he had a friend willing and able to help him do that, all the better.

And nothing's worse than not living up to your own expectations.

Dear God, what had he expected of himself? No human being could be expected to hold out against such torture. How could he blame himself?

She couldn't bear the thought of it. That alone should have told her how far gone she was, but she was already moving, on her way to find him, hoping she could think of something to say to make him see the absurdity of this particular male notion of honor, or whatever it was.

If she hadn't been in such a hurry to say her piece, it never would have happened. But she was, and it did; she tapped on his door, in her urgency rather harder than she usually would have, and it swung open.

He was standing there in nothing but a towel, his back to her as he looked over his shoulder at the door she'd inadvertently opened. His back bore more scars, including a patch that looked as if it had once been badly burned, and more recently damaged somehow. The fight, she thought rather numbly. That was where he'd been bleeding.

But that was all the time she spent dwelling on the marks on his body, because he spoke then.

''If you came to join me in the shower, you're a bit late.''

His voice sounded harsh, tight. She felt herself color, and struggled for a casual quip, some joke that would make light of the embarrassing situation. Instead what came out was something that shocked even her.

"Too bad for me."

She heard him suck in an audible breath. He seemed to hesitate, then turned to face her.

"I'm in no mood for jokes, Emma." She could see that. The towel didn't do much to hide exactly what kind of mood he was in.

"Neither am I," she said, her voice suddenly husky at the idea that this fierce-looking physical response was for her.

"Then I'm the only one dressed for the occasion," he pointed out, clearly thinking she wasn't serious.

Well, she wasn't serious. Was she?

The answer to that question thrummed through her body. She'd never felt anything like this before, and while the cautious side of her wanted to run, the rest of her was crying out that she might never feel like this again.

She would never do this at home, she thought. But then, she never would have stayed voluntarily aboard a boat, either. This place had begun to work some sort of magic on her from the moment her flight had entered the air space over Puget Sound.

"Emma?" he said softly, as if he could tell she was teetering and was afraid to say anything more.

"I guess I should change, then," she said huskily, her hands going to the hem of her sweater.

He swore, low, harsh and deep. He took one quick step forward and grabbed her wrists. "Don't start this if you don't intend to finish it. I'm too close to the edge."

"I'll start it," she said, not even trying to pull free, "but I'm hoping you'll finish it."

With a low groan he pulled her into his arms. His mouth took hers with a fierceness and speed that took her breath away. It was everything she'd remembered from the first time, but with one distinct difference; this time he kissed her like he would never stop. And she realized, in the moment before a swelling wave of pleasure swept away thought, that was exactly it. This time he wouldn't be stopping. And that sent her heart racing, spreading the heat from his mouth even faster. Unable to stop herself, she reached for him. Felt the heat of him in the moment before her fingers touched his skin.

She felt him stiffen as her fingertips brushed over the raised ridge of a scar. She broke the kiss, reluctantly, but this was more important. She bent to press her lips to his chest, over the scar, and let her tongue flick out to trace the line of it.

He shuddered beneath the liquid caress, and as she felt it go through him she nearly gasped at the sensation of power that flooded her. She'd never felt that way before, never knew it was possible. Oh, she knew on other levels the satisfaction of giving pleasure, but she had never experienced anything like this.

It could, she thought, become addictive. She traced a path of nibbling little kisses from the scar to a flat male nipple, wondering if he would react if she did the same there. She did, and he did.

"Emma."

It came out through clenched teeth, which only added to her sense of power. It was heady stuff for an unsophisticated woman like her. Definitely addictive.

"If you don't get rid of some of your clothes, I will,

and I can't promise they'll be wearable when I'm done.''

It was both promise and passionate threat, and Emma suddenly realized that hers wasn't the only power here. ''Go ahead,'' she said, shivering at the thought of him undressing her. None of the very few men she'd ever been with had made her feel like this.

He didn't ask her again, didn't give her a chance to change her mind. Not that she wanted one. And true to his word he yanked at her sweater, tugging it over her head with a haste that flattered her. For a moment then he fumbled with the fastening of her bra, and she felt oddly pleased that he didn't do it so nimbly it would make her wonder how often he'd done it before.

Finally he gave up with a near snarl of frustration and instead pulled the stretchy fabric from the front— with exquisite care—until her breasts slipped free. Then he tugged it over her head and tossed it, still fastened, as he had the sweater.

He let out a low, prayerful exclamation as he slowly reached up to cup her breasts. She nearly cried out for him to hurry; she wanted his hands on her so badly it stunned her. She'd never felt this ache before, an ache that nearly made her moan aloud with need.

And then he touched her, delicately, reverently, and she did moan. And leaned slightly, into his hands, silently urging him to do more. He cupped her aching flesh, lifted. Her nipples tightened, achingly, and it was all she could do to keep from begging him to touch her there.

''Is this what you want?'' he asked softly in the moment before he rubbed the taut peaks with his thumbs.

''Yes,'' she gasped out as fire flashed through her.

When he bent and replaced his fingers with his

mouth, she cried out at the shock of sensation that jolted through her. She grabbed at him blindly, catching his shoulders by luck, as he drew first one nipple, then the other deeply into his mouth and flicked it repeatedly with his tongue.

Her back arched involuntarily, a convulsive motion that thrust her breasts toward him harder. She barely noticed when her feet left the floor, only realizing when she felt rich plush beneath her back that he had lifted her onto his bed. For an instant she tried to be embarrassed; she was no lightweight, after all, but all she could manage was to be glad he was strong enough to do it.

He came down beside her, and she realized he'd either discarded the towel or it had fallen away. She couldn't stop herself from staring. His body had the lean, ropy kind of muscle that spoke of great fitness, and that he still had so much after what he'd been through told her what kind of incredible shape he must have been in before. And then her gaze slid downward, and she couldn't think at all. Obviously, no matter what had been done to the rest of him, one part was clearly in perfect working order.

Lord, she was really going to do this. But she wasn't prepared. This had been the very last thing on her mind when she'd come here, and since her love life had been pretty skimpy for the past year or two, she wasn't ready with any protection.

When she realized he was watching her look at him, she felt heat rise in her face and she turned her head away. He caught her with a gentle finger under her chin and turned her back to face him, then shook his head.

"I've been wanting this for so long, don't go shy on me now."

"I'm not. I won't. I just…haven't done much of this. I'm not…prepared."

"Lately neither have I," he said dryly. "But I think…" He rolled over and dug into a drawer in a bedside table and came up with a foil packet. "This has on occasion," he said with a lopsided grin, "been the honeymoon suite."

Relieved that the problem had been resolved so easily, Emma tried to relax. She would have thought the brief pause would have given her time for second thoughts, but somehow the fact that Harlan had realized her worry and solved it only made her more certain this was right for her. At least, for right now.

He took care of the protection now, muttering that he wouldn't trust himself to do it later. And then he turned back to her, and began where he'd left off. Emma's body rose to his touch, until her skin seemed to be tingling even where he wasn't touching. Not that there was a place he didn't get around to eventually.

He told her she was beautiful, he told her she tasted sweet, he told her everything she'd ever wanted to hear. And when at last he nudged her legs apart and slid into her, he told her how she fit him in one word.

"Perfect," he said, his voice a low, gravelly rumble now.

Emma couldn't find words at all. The gloriously full sensation was too much, and all she could do was moan her pleasure and hope he understood. He seemed to, because every time he moved in a way that made her gasp or quiver he did it again. And again, until she was clutching him wildly. Yet still she wanted more. She wanted it wilder, deeper, fiercer.

He began to move faster, until she cried out. He froze. "Too much?"

"No," she said urgently. "Oh, no. More."

As if that was all he needed to hear he gave her exactly what she wanted. He drove hard and deep, again and again. She arched to meet him, crying out his name, and he slipped his hands beneath her hips to lift her. Just that change in angle made her cry out again, and her fingers dug into his shoulders as he slammed into her yet again.

"Emma," he gasped out. "I can't…I'm sorry…"

She didn't know what he was talking about. At this instant she didn't care. She could feel her body gathering for flight, a body that had already experienced more in these heated moments than it ever had before.

And then Harlan lowered his head to her breast, caught a nipple with his lips and sucked it into his mouth urgently. That burst of heat shot through her to blend with the fire already raging, and in that moment she convulsed almost violently, her body arching upward as his name broke from her in a cry she couldn't stop as wave after wave of sensation crashed over her.

A low, guttural groan vibrated up from his chest and she felt him shudder as his body drove into hers and this time stayed. He ground his hips against her, as if he wanted to climb inside, and each movement sent another ripple of pleasure through her.

Emma cradled him in her arms, heard him murmur her name, softly this time, and as the incredible heat ebbed she knew that no matter what happened now— or didn't—she could never regret this decision. No matter how shocked she was at her own passion.

Fourteen

The sound of footsteps on the dock woke him. He didn't think much of it—after the night they'd spent he could barely think at all—until he remembered the burglary. His eyes shot open; it was morning. Late morning, he realized with a glance at the clock. Emma was curled up beside him, her long legs tangled with his, and he was loathe to move at all.

And then the steady, even footsteps stopped. If he was hearing right, they had stopped right at the steps to the *Seahawk*. He sat up.

"Ahoy, the *Seahawk!*"

Damn, Harlan thought as he recognized the voice. This was the last thing he would have expected.

He rolled out of bed as quickly as he could without waking Emma. He pulled on jeans and a T-shirt, grabbed a pair of battered deck shoes, and tiptoed barefoot to the door. Once he had it closed behind him he tugged on the shoes and headed up on deck.

Even though he'd recognized the voice, it still surprised him to see the tall, lanky man leaning against the railing. The cool gray eyes took in his tousled appearance, but he said only, "Permission to come aboard?"

Harlan's mouth quirked. "You have to ask?"

"It's only polite," the man drawled.

"Mi barco es su barco," Harlan said with an elaborate bow as he gestured the visitor aboard. "Or do I have that backwards?"

"It works both ways," the man drawled again as he came aboard.

"I'll put coffee on."

He trusted no comment would be made on the late hour for starting coffee, and he was right. The rich, dark liquid began to drip into the pot, and he turned around and leaned against the counter.

"Just thought I'd see how you were doing."

"You happened to be in the neighborhood?" Harlan asked wryly; headquarters was twelve hundred miles away in Southern California.

"Out for some R and R before a meeting in Seattle."

"Meaning flying."

"What else?" The grin was quick.

"Where'd you come in?"

"Port Angeles. I wanted to drive over the Hood Canal Bridge."

"Well, that sounds like you," Harlan said with a grin.

"And you look a hell of a lot better than when I last saw you."

Harlan shrugged. "I'm getting by."

"This place must agree with you."

"You said it would. It's…distracting enough." *And how,* Harlan added silently, thinking of the woman still sleeping below.

"Have you talked to Dr. Sims lately?"

"No." Harlan grimaced at the shrink's name. "I'd rather just get through it than spill my guts to her anymore."

"Can't say as I blame you on that."

"It's getting better," Harlan said. "I—"

He cut himself off as he heard footsteps approaching from below. *Here it comes,* he thought. He tried to be philosophical about it, this had been, he supposed, inevitable, but the timing was a bit dicey, coming on the heels of their first night together.

"Harlan?"

Emma's voice still sounded sleepy, but when she topped the steps and saw they had company he saw her wake up in a rush.

"Oh. Sorry, I didn't know—"

"It's all right, Emma," Harlan said. "Meet the owner of the *Seahawk.*"

"Oh." She blinked. "Oh!"

"Josh, meet Emma Purcell. She's the not-so-lucky owner of that tub at the end of the dock."

"The sailboat? My condolences."

Emma smiled ruefully. "Accepted." She hesitated, her forehead creasing as she looked at the man offering his hand. But then she smiled back and shook it.

"Nice to meet you. You have a lovely boat here."

"There are bigger and fancier, but I like her," he said.

Harlan watched Emma, wondering if she'd take offense at the traditional feminine terminology. If she did, not a flicker of it showed.

"You mean you have a soft spot for her, since she was the first boat you designed," Harlan pointed out.

"That, too." The easy admission came with a lazy grin.

"You designed the boat yourself?" Emma asked.

Josh only nodded, so Harlan added, "Not bad for a guy used to building airplanes."

"Airplanes?" Emma's brow furrowed again, and then, suddenly cleared. Recognition flashed across her face. "Oh, my God. You're Josh Redstone!"

"Guilty," Josh said, with that sort of smothered sigh that Harlan knew was Josh's way of preparing himself for people he met to start acting differently once they knew who he was.

It wasn't surprising she recognized him. Josh was, after all, world famous for many reasons, not the least of which were the sleek, powerful private jets built by Redstone Aviation, and the advances made possible by Redstone Technologies. But he was, in addition to being a self-made billionaire several times over, also known worldwide for his generosity. His criteria was simple; he believed in giving a hand up, not handouts, and anybody who was willing to work as hard as Josh himself did could count on his help.

And as if the thought was emblazoned on her forehead, he knew that was what she was thinking, about Josh's charity, when her gaze flicked to him then back to Josh. He half expected her to say something about him sponging off Josh for too long.

"I'm sorry," she said instead, sounding utterly genuine. "That must happen to you a lot when you meet people."

Josh smiled then, and his gray eyes warmed slightly.

"It does. It's natural, I guess. I have a much higher profile than I would like."

"In a better way than some," Emma pointed out.

"Than too many," he agreed.

She seemed to study Josh for a moment, as if trying to decide whether to say something. He lifted a brow in encouragement, and at last she spoke.

"You know how you think of what you'd do or say if you ever met somebody famous?" Looking suddenly wary, Josh nodded. "Well, I always thought that if I ever met you, I'd say thank you."

"For what?"

She smiled. "For existing. As the kind of man you are."

Josh blinked. Swallowed.

"Congratulations, Emma," Harlan said with a grin, "you got him."

Recovering, Josh smiled at her. "That's quite a compliment. Nicest I've had in a long while."

Emma slid Harlan a sideways look, and he wasn't sure if she was impressed that he knew Josh Redstone, or upset that this was the man whose charity he was taking.

"Sometimes maybe you're too generous," she said.

"Oh?" Josh asked.

"Emma's been worried about you," Harlan said, a bit sourly.

"Worried?"

"Well, upset on your behalf, I guess. She thinks I'm sponging off you. Before she knew it was you, of course. Now that she knows, I think she's even more upset."

Josh looked at Emma with bemusement; Emma's cheeks were fiery red, and Harlan knew he'd pay for this later. But he'd known her concern would make Josh like her even more, and that was important to him. And the moment that realization registered, his mind skittered away from it.

"Well, now, that's an interesting thought," Josh said, his drawl more exaggerated than usual, which Harlan knew meant that agile mind hidden behind the laid-back exterior was racing.

He shifted his gaze to Harlan, who knew Josh must have guessed he'd not told Emma anything. He also knew Josh was no fool, and after seeing them both emerge from below tousled and sleepy, especially with Emma looking like a woman who had been thoroughly loved, Harlan knew he'd add it up correctly. Josh hadn't gotten to where he was by being blind.

"Is there a reason?" Josh asked softly.

Harlan didn't pretend not to understand. "Pride," he admitted wryly.

"Well, then."

Josh turned back to a clearly puzzled Emma, and Harlan knew he was going to tell her. He didn't really mind. It was time.

"I appreciate your concern, Emma. It's been a long time since anyone outside the Redstone family has worried about me like that. But this guy has never sponged off me. Or anyone else, for that matter."

"I didn't exactly say—"

She stopped when Josh held up a hand. "In fact," he went on, "if anything it's the other way around. Redstone wouldn't exist if it wasn't for him. He's the man who had the vision to invest in a country boy who had nothing but a pilot's license and an idea."

Emma gaped at Josh, then at Harlan as Josh continued.

"He's a cornerstone of Redstone Incorporated. Even though he's busy tracking his own investments around the world, he's still my right hand financial mentor, and purely a genius. But won't even take a salary. Not that he needs it, but he certainly earns it."

"I keep your money working, it makes more for me," Harlan said easily.

Emma seemed stunned, sank into a chair, and lapsed into silence. His point made, Josh chatted amiably for a while longer before rising and saying he needed to catch the next ferry to get to his meeting. He gave Emma a gracious goodbye, and thanked her again for her concern, to which she responded as if still stunned.

Harlan walked with Josh to the door.

"Take care, Mac," Josh said. "We need you back. And there's that site off Grand Cayman that's still calling."

Harlan nodded, feeling the weight of Josh's concern. His friend's eyes always held a shadow, but now it was darker than ever.

When he walked back inside, Emma was staring at him as if she'd never seen him before. His chest tightened. He'd been afraid of this, afraid once she knew he wasn't the marina bum she'd thought, that things would change somehow.

Abruptly she got up. "I need to get to work."

She walked to the sink, rinsed out her mug, turned on her heel and left without another word.

And Harlan found himself recalling why being around Josh always reminded him it was never wise to fall in love too deeply. Josh had, and when his wife had died she'd taken his heart and a big piece of his spirit with her.

He just hoped the recollection hadn't come too late to save his own heart.

* * *

Mac. Joshua Redstone had called him Mac, and ten seconds later she'd felt like the biggest fool on earth.

Mac. Mac McClaren.

It wasn't enough, she thought as she clenched her teeth and pushed the sanding block harder, that she'd misjudged him entirely, although her thinking he was a bum and a sponger alone would be enough to make anyone laugh hysterically. No, she had to miss the totally obvious, what half the world would probably have realized in the first instant of hearing his name.

How many clues did she need, for heaven's sake? She had his name. That he'd been all over the world. That he'd lived his whole life on boats.

Mac McClaren. World famous treasure hunter. The man who had made his fortune—enough for several fortunes—at age twenty-two when he found the sunken Spanish galleon his late father had spent years searching for. She'd even seen a picture of him before, in a magazine, as she recalled. But he'd been one man surrounded by his exultant crew, and she hadn't taken any particular notice.

One of the richest men in the country, and you convince yourself he's a bum, sponging off a man who turns out to be one of the richest men in the world. You are really something, she told herself with an inward groan.

Maybe he'd had a reason for not telling her who he really was. Maybe his wealth alone was reason enough. He probably had people climbing all over him wanting money. She sighed, remembering what she'd told him about money troubles, a normal thing to discuss—unless you were talking to a gazillionaire.

And to top it off, she felt like a coward for taking off like that this morning. After the night they'd shared, surely he deserved more?

She shivered at the memories that flooded her then, of his hands, his mouth, and what they'd done to her, made her do. And what she'd done to him as well, following his every hint of what he'd like and finding more pleasure in that than she'd ever thought possible.

She lasted only a few more minutes before she gave up. She threw down the sanding block and paper, dusted herself off as best she could, and clambered down the steps—she still hung on to the rail tightly—to the dock. She headed back to the *Seahawk*—Josh Redstone's boat, she thought incredulously. Never in a million years would she have thought she'd even meet the man, let alone be virtually living on one of his boats.

But he'd been nice, she thought. More down to earth than she would have expected, despite all the stories that emphasized that quality.

And Harlan had given him his start. She'd read somewhere he'd been backed by another risk taker as adventurous as he himself, but she'd not heard or read that it had been the reckless Mac McClaren.

She hesitated in the act of setting foot on the deck of the *Seahawk*, still not quite able to believe it. She needed time, she thought. Time to get her mind around this. Josh hadn't actually told her who Harlan really was, she'd finally—belatedly—put that together herself. So she could simply not let on she finally knew who he was, until she'd had time to figure out if—and how— it changed things.

Feeling a bit better now, she boarded and went in search of the man who had not only found a sunken treasure, but apparently provided the foundation for one of the biggest international corporations in the world.

She found him in his computer room, a room that now made a lot more sense to her. He probably needed every bit of this equipment to track his own small empire.

"I'm sorry I ran like that," she blurted to his back.

He froze, then slowly turned around. The look on his face was so guarded she winced.

"I just needed some time to…absorb, I guess."

"Like me better as a bum?"

"Wayne's the one who said it first, in his letter," she said, knowing she was sounding defensive.

"I know. And I just fulfilled the prophecy, didn't I?"

"Well, you didn't go out of your way to convince me otherwise," she said, recapturing a bit of her resentment at having been made a fool.

"I know. And I'm sorry about that. Now. At the time, it seemed…the thing to do."

She took a deep breath and decided to jump in feet first. "Afraid I'd come asking for money?"

"People do."

She was glad he didn't deny it. And she only now realized that her story about Safe Haven could have sounded like a plea for money, to a man who had it. That he'd had doubts about her somewhat eased her guilt about her early suspicions of him. "I imagine you have to be careful," she said.

"Not as careful as Josh. He's easier to find." One corner of his mouth quirked upward. "You impressed him. Worrying about him being taken advantage of."

She flushed. "Maybe I impressed him with how wrong I was."

Harlan, or Mac, shook his head. "One thing about

Josh. Behind that country boy drawl is a mind like a rocket scientist, and it's got a built-in bull detector. He's real good at assessing people.''

"Is he ever wrong?''

"He has been, but not often.'' He gave her a long, steady look. "And I don't think he's wrong this time.''

Emma's color deepened, but with pleasure this time. And as the day went on and they worked in their old companionable silence, the more she thought about it the more she could understand why he'd not announced his identity up front. And really, he hadn't lied to her, he'd given her his real name, and simply not told her anything that would have made her think anything other than what she'd been set up to believe. Obviously he knew what the general perception of him was around here, and he didn't care. It was probably beneficial, in fact, a buffer against the kind of people who really were what he was pretending to be.

It wasn't until after they'd eaten a simple dinner of grilled salmon and an avocado salad that Harlan brought up the subject that had been niggling at her since this morning's revelations. His voice was quiet, but it rattled her as much as if he'd shouted.

"I never thanked you for last night.''

"I didn't give you much chance,'' she admitted. "But…you don't need to. The other way around, maybe. I should thank you.''

He smiled then, the warmest smile she'd seen from him all day. "Are we all right, then? I was thinking you might still be mad.''

"I don't think I was really mad. Embarrassed, feeling foolish, yes.''

"Don't. There was no reason for you not to believe what you did. But,'' he added, a note of unease coming into his voice, "I should have told you the truth before last night."

"Yes," she said, surprised at her own calm. "But if you had, last night might not have happened."

He blinked. "Why?"

"Because I would have been afraid you would have thought that was the reason, because you're…rich. That that was why I gave in to what I was feeling."

His voice went suddenly harsh as he pinned her with his gaze. "And what were you feeling?"

With an effort, she met that sharp look. "I wasn't sure. I just knew I'd never felt that kind of wanting before."

He made a low sound that sent a shiver through her. "Lord, woman, you take a man's breath away."

"Turnabout and all that," she retorted.

He looked at her for a long, silent moment before saying, "I try not to make assumptions, Emma. So now, you're going to have to make the first move."

It took her a moment to realize what he meant. It made her feel good that he wasn't assuming they would be together tonight, that he felt he should ask. Things *had* changed, and she took this as evidence he knew it, and was giving her the choice all over again. Not that there was any doubt in her mind. Not after last night.

"Where would you like me to start?" she asked huskily.

He told her, in terms graphic enough to make her blush, but in a voice tortured enough to make her ache to do exactly as he asked. And the moment they got to his stateroom, she began. She undressed him slowly, then undressed herself, unable to quite believe she was doing it with his hot eyes on her. And then she draped herself over him until they were skin to skin head to toe, just as he'd wanted.

She began the kind of slow, heated caresses he'd used to drive her to the brink of madness last night. She only hoped she could quickly learn him as well as he had learned her. She savored every gasp, every groan that broke from him, and memorized the touch and the place that had evoked it. And at last, when he choked out her name and begged her to end it, she reached for his rigid flesh and eased herself down on it in a slow impalement that made them both moan with the intensity of it.

No matter how fast or urgently she moved, he urged her to more, until they were both wild with it. When he grabbed her hips to bring her down hard on him, she cried out at the luscious impact, and then again as her body erupted. Through the haze enveloping her she heard him call out her name, felt his muscles clench, his body arch beneath her.

Still trembling, her nerves still sending little pulses of pleasure along seared pathways, she collapsed atop him. He groaned, but his arms came around her and pulled her even harder against him.

"Emma?" he finally said, after several minutes had passed.

"Mmm." It was all she could manage.

"We gotta talk." He wasn't doing much better, it seemed.

"'morrow."

She thought she felt him smile. "'kay."

She fell asleep before she could wonder what he would say tomorrow.

It didn't matter. At 3:00 a.m. the world seemed to erupt around them, and they woke to the echo of an explosion, the sound of shattering glass and the sting and smell of smoke.

Fifteen

Harlan swore, low and harsh, as he stared at what was left of the *Pretty Lady.*

"If you'd been on board, you'd be dead," he said, his voice tight.

"I wasn't," Emma said, and he marveled at her calm. But maybe it wasn't calm, maybe she was in shock. He turned her around to look at her face, but she seemed fine. "I wasn't," she repeated. "I was safe. Very safe." She looked up at him then. "Thank you, Mac."

She knew who he was. He saw it in her eyes then, but it didn't matter to him. Nothing did as memories of the hot, sweet night flooded him, and he suddenly realized how she could be so calm. After what they'd found together, it would take a lot to rattle him, too. Unfortunately this threat to her, even though she'd escaped it, definitely fell into that category. And he no longer cared what that said about the state of his entanglement with her.

The firefighters were still hurrying around, although the fire boat they'd summoned had left when it was determined they could do no more. The *Pretty Lady* was gone, burned to the waterline and already awash.

"Must have been a vapor or fume buildup, under the deck," the man with the hard hat labeled "A.I." said. Harlan guessed it meant Arson Investigator, not Artificial Intelligence. "That engine looks pretty thrashed, like it hadn't been maintained at all."

"It probably hasn't been," Emma agreed, "but that's not what happened."

The man looked at her curiously. "Oh?"

She proceeded to tell him about the burglary, and Harlan saw the reassessment going on in the man's mind as if it were tangible.

"We'll contact the sheriff's office right away," he promised. "In the meantime, the sooner you can get a crane here to get what's left of it out of there, the less it'll cost you."

Here at least, was something he could do, Harlan thought. He got his cell phone and began making calls, invoking the Redstone name and his own money to get someone out here before noon. By the time he hung up the sheriff's deputy had arrived, and although she agreed it was suspicious coming on the heels of the burglary, Harlan could tell she thought it could just as easily be the all too common result of a neglected, run-down marine engine. But they would investigate, the deputy promised.

"I know it wasn't an accident," Emma said when they were alone again.

"I agree," he said mildly. He slipped an arm around

her shoulders. "I just don't believe in that much coincidence."

She seemed relieved. "What do you think happened?"

"If I had to guess, I'd say our friends gave up on finding what they were looking for and decided to just destroy it instead."

She nodded as she stared down at the still smoking ruin. "That's what I thought."

"Come on. There's no point in staring at it. We'll come back when the salvage crane gets here."

After a moment she agreed and they walked back to the *Seahawk.* He fixed some lunch more as a distraction than out of hunger, but to his surprise they actually finished it. And by then the crane had arrived, and they went back outside to oversee the operation.

It took the operators some time to set up their rigging and a sling around what was left of the *Pretty Lady,* so it was over an hour before what was left of her was finally lifted out of the water. Once they were sure it was stable, the crane crew prepared to swing the wreckage over to the barge. It was at that moment that something caught Harlan's eye. He waved the crew to a halt.

"What's that?" he asked, leaning forward to stare at the dripping hulk.

"What?" Emma asked.

"There. On the side of the keel."

"You mean that thing that looks like a patch?"

"Yeah. It wasn't there when I dove the hull for him, so it has to be fresh."

"And sloppy," the salvage man put in as he joined them on the dock. "Real amateur work."

"Now why," Harlan wondered aloud, "would he do a thing like that, when the keel was fine?"

It was curious enough that when the crane lowered what was left of the hull to the deck of the barge, Harlan asked permission to board and take a look. Emma's newly developed comfort zone on the water didn't extend to industrial-looking barges, so she stayed on the dock.

Once he was close enough, Harlan could see that the patch was indeed fresh. And when he leaned over to look at it from a different angle, something about the thickness of the patch bothered him. He asked for a knife, and was handed a rather lethal-looking blade by the crane operator. It didn't take long for him to discover the patch was nothing more than a rectangle of plastic heavily taped down and then painted to match the keel. He kept digging with the blade, until he had one corner free.

Certain now there was something here, he kept tugging, until the blade finally sliced neatly through the painted plastic. He stood staring at what was revealed, a small packet of papers wrapped in heavy plastic. And for an instant he wished he'd left well enough alone. He didn't want Emma involved in this anymore, not when there were guys out there willing to do whatever it took to get what they wanted. And what they wanted was now right in front of him, he had no doubt of that.

"What is it?" Emma called out from the dock.

He had to show her, he thought. She had the right to know, even if he'd like nothing better than to burn whatever this was unread, and let the guys who had done this assume they'd succeeded.

Wishing he had a choice, he worked the papers free, returned the knife to the now curious crane operator, and climbed off the barge. Emma was waiting, watching him with a very intent expression.

The first words out of her mouth startled him. "It's what Wayne said, isn't it?"

"What?"

"He said, in his note, 'She holds her secrets deep, but they're there.' That the *Pretty Lady* would have the answer."

Only then did he remember that phrase in the letter Wayne had mailed to her the day before he'd died. "The answer to what, though," he muttered as they headed back to the *Seahawk* to deal with this. Whatever it was, he had a feeling it was not going to be good.

Back in the *Seahawk*'s main salon, they opened the packet. Inside were several sheets of paper that looked as if they'd been torn out of a ledger, and another small envelope with Emma's name on it. They spread the papers out on the big table. The page of columns with initials, dates, other numbers and what appeared to be locations meant nothing obvious to either of them.

Harlan looked at Emma. She was staring at the small envelope they'd as yet not opened. He could see in her face she had the same feeling he did, that the answer was in there. And that it was an answer she might not want to see.

He saw the moment when she braced herself, and a second later she reached for the envelope. As if now that she'd decided to do it, she wanted it done, she tore it open with a determination he admired. As he admired so much about her. She'd battled her fear of water, of boats, and come to terms with it. She'd adjusted her view of her beloved cousin when the evidence became overwhelming. She'd accepted his little deception, even understanding one of the reasons he'd done it before he'd explained it. And now she was wading into what was surely going to be an ugly mess, simply because it had to be done.

There was a lot to admire about Emma Purcell. She was the kind of woman who would deal with whatever life threw at her, in the best way she could. The kind of woman a man could look long and hard to find. The kind of woman—

He cut off his own thoughts when he realized they were heading in a direction he'd never gone, never even imagined going before. And yet he didn't feel the urge to dodge, the urge to shy away from the very idea—

"Oh, God…"

The distress in her voice snapped him out of his reverie. She was staring at the note in her hand, scrawled in the same hand he recognized from Wayne's earlier letter. As he looked at her she let it fall to the table, then buried her face in her hands.

He didn't even hesitate in grabbing the page. If it hurt Emma, it was his business, and he'd deal with the ramifications of that later.

He wanted to groan himself when he read Wayne's note. This was his idea of "taking care" of his cousin?

If you weren't already dead, I'd be tempted, he thought grimly.

"I can't believe it," she said, and he suspected she was crying, or close to it. "How could he do this? How could he even think I would ever use this?"

"His brain was fried, Emma. I doubt he was thinking at all."

"But it's so…twisted! How could he think I'd be *glad* to get a list of some scummy drug dealers and their clients, that I'd follow his instructions and use it to blackmail them?"

Because it's what he would have done, Harlan

thought. But it was unnecessary to say; the last of her illusions had clearly been shattered, there was no point in grinding the bits into the dirt.

"Maybe he really thought this was his best shot at taking care of you," he suggested, trying not to grimace at the irony of now being the one to defend her dead cousin to her.

"Some legacy. Nice to know what he thought worthy of me." She pushed the papers away, as if she couldn't bear to be that close to them. Harlan figured at this point he'd said enough; this was something she was going to have to work through herself, and all he could do was be there.

She stared at the note he'd dropped back on top of the other papers for a very long time. At last she looked up at him with eyes so bleak they tore at his heart.

"Do you think he could have been killed for these? That maybe it wasn't an accident after all?"

Harlan opened his mouth to say no, but then stopped. She deserved honesty now, especially since he'd been less than forthright with her before. "Maybe," he conceded. "He obviously knew somebody would come looking for them, or he wouldn't have gone to so much trouble to hide them."

Her mouth tightened into a pained line as she lowered her gaze to the damning papers on the table once more. "I'd just as soon burn them. But I can't help thinking I should hand them over to the police."

"They'd be glad to get it, I'm sure," he said neutrally.

"Still, even after all this, I hate the idea of dragging his name through the mud even more. But if they killed him, I hate the idea of them getting away with it."

Harlan watched her troubled expression for a moment, knowing that if he started this, there would be no turning back. Then she lifted her eyes to his, and he knew there was no "if" about it.

"There's another way."

"What?"

"That man who pulled me out of the jungle."

Her forehead creased. "What about him?"

"He has friends in many, many places. Friends who would be glad to get this kind of intel with no questions asked. And who wouldn't be at all surprised that he had it."

"He'd keep Wayne's name out of it?"

"If that's how you want it."

"But he doesn't even know me."

"Josh will vouch for you. That'll be enough for Draven. And he'll see the men on that list are dealt with appropriately."

"Just like that?"

"The power of Redstone," Harlan said.

For a long moment she just looked at him, and he could almost see her agile mind working, considering. At last, she nodded. "All right." Then, as he gathered up the papers, she said, "You know, I've always heard of Redstone. Didn't know if I should believe half of what I heard. It seemed too good to be true."

"It's good, and it's true. Josh sees to that."

"And you?"

He shook his head. "I just go about my business and let my investment pay for what I want to do."

"Treasure hunting."

He nodded. "You have a problem with that?"

"Not nearly the problem I had with thinking I was falling for a marina bum," she admitted with the blunt honesty he loved. And then, belatedly, he realized what she'd just admitted to.

"You…fell for me?"

She sighed. "In a big way."

He swallowed tightly. There was no longer any doubt that she'd broken through the shell of weariness that had surrounded him since he'd come here. In fact, she'd shattered that shell, leaving him freer and lighter than he'd felt in what seemed like forever.

"Do you have any idea what that means to me? That who I am, what I am, had nothing to do with it?" It was the best gift she could ever have given him.

"I'm not sure what it means to you, period," she said, her tone dry.

He hadn't, he realized suddenly, properly responded to her admission. And since he'd never done this before, he wasn't at all sure how to go about it. Finally, he settled on the thing he guessed would mean the most to her.

"You know, I've been thinking I need a dog."

She blinked. "What?"

"A dog. Maybe a grown one, to start with. Puppy later."

"I…see." She looked uncertain, as if she suspected there was another level to his words, but not sure what it was.

"I'll need help, of course. Lots of training." He gave her a sideways look and a lopsided grin. "Me, I mean."

"I see," she repeated, but she was smiling now.

"Know anybody who might be willing to help? I could relocate, move…oh, maybe way south, if it would help. Redstone's there, after all. Maybe I could even spend some time ashore, if I could see the water."

"That's…quite a concession."

"There'd have to be some turnabout, though."

"You mean someone willing to spend some time on the water?"

He nodded. "And someone who understands what I have to do with my life. As I would understand what they had to do with theirs."

"I think," Emma said slowly, "it takes someone with a passion of their own to understand someone else with one."

The simple statement resonated with him in the manner of a revelation. "Yes," he said, wondering why he'd never thought of it that way before.

"Not," she added with a grimace, "that anyone would understand trekking through a Central American jungle."

"No more of that. I'm sticking to the sea, where I know my way around."

"Well, then. In that case, I might know someone who'd be willing to try," she said, a smile tugging at the corners of her mouth. "If you go gently with her, about the water thing. Start out slow."

"I can do that," he promised. Then, with a glint in his eye, he added a warning. "She should know that Redstone throws a wicked wedding."

She blinked. "Wedding?"

Harlan shrugged. "No rush. Just advance notice."

Much later, lying in Harlan's arms, Emma spoke softly. "You know, unintentionally, Wayne actually gave me a priceless gift."

"Now that you put it that way," Harlan said as he nuzzled her hair, "I may have to forgive him. Because he gave it to me, too."

Epilogue

Emma laughed joyously at the sight before her; her soon to be husband, trying hard to look sternly at the soaking wet, tongue-lolling chocolate Labrador retriever who had just clambered up on the dock where Harlan's new boat was moored and shaken her coatload of sea water all over him. But she looked up at him as she always did, from beneath lowered brows, pitifully, as if she just knew he was about to stomp on her heart.

And as he always did, Harlan burst out laughing. He knelt down and, despite the sogginess, hugged the delighted dog he'd appropriately named Splash. She spread a little more water around with her frantically wagging tail.

It had taken Emma a few inquiries and some help from the delighted and astounded Sheila, to find the perfect rescue dog for Harlan's gift. She'd had to take her right away, long before the wedding, but it had taken the water and boat-loving Splash all of a couple of days to worm her way into Harlan's heart. She was definitely a McClaren now. As Emma would soon be. Much to her parents' shock and Sheila's delight.

"Don't worry," she said to man and dog with a chuckle she couldn't hold back, "you're in Southern California now, you'll dry quickly."

"You can laugh," Harlan said with mock sternness as he stood up, "but she soaked your wedding present."

"What?"

He pulled an envelope out of his coat pocket and handed it to her. "I meant to do it better, maybe over champagne, but you'd better read it quick, before it soaks through."

Curious then, she opened the manila envelope and pulled out the sheaf of papers. It took a moment to register, but once it did, she gaped at him. "Is this what it looks like?"

"I sure hope so. Otherwise I spent a lot of time charming that old man for nothing."

"Mr. Kean? He actually sold it to you?"

"That he did," Harlan said with unmistakable satisfaction.

Emma stared, unable to quite believe she now owned the land Safe Haven sat on. They were safe, the animals were safe. She looked at Harlan, but before she could open her mouth he stopped her with a kiss.

"Don't mess with me about this, Emma. I wanted to do it. And get used to it. I plan to buy you lots of things."

"As long as it's things like this, and not silly jewelry and stuff like that."

"Yes, ma'am," he said. "We'll build the best shelter any animal could want."

They'd had this discussion in depth, and had reached, she thought, a decent accord. She would keep her dream. With his help it was now a certainty, and she could even relax and go away with him now and then. And he would keep his own dream, following the wind from place to place, indulging in the passion for treasure hunting that had made him famous, but now he would have a home base to always return to. Somehow they would build a life around both dreams.

"No arguing about the honeymoon, either," he reminded her. "Josh wanted to do it, and there's no stopping the man when his mind's set."

Although the idea of flying in a luxury private jet to wherever her heart desired, for however long, still amazed her, she couldn't deny she was excited. She threw her arms around the man she'd finally said yes to and kissed him soundly, heedless of the fact that now she, too, was soaked.

Splash danced around their feet, tail still doing a happy wave. She'd landed in doggy heaven, and she knew it. Emma just smiled, in her own kind of heaven, one that would last forever.

*   *   *   *   *

Silhouette® Desire®

presents

DYNASTIES: THE DANFORTHS

**A family of prominence...
tested by scandal, sustained by passion!**

Man Beneath the Uniform
by
MAUREEN CHILD
(Silhouette Desire #1561)

He was her protector. But navy SEAL
Zachary Sheriday wanted to be more
than just a bodyguard to sexy scientist
Kimberly Danforth. Was this one seduction
Zachary was duty-bound to deny...?

*Available February 2004
at your favorite retail outlet.*

Visit Silhouette at www.eHarlequin.com   SDDYNMBTU

Silhouette

Desire®

presents

The Long Hot Summer
(#1565)
by
ROCHELLE ALERS

It is the sizzling first title of a brand-new series

THE
BLACKSTONES
OF VIRGINIA

Ryan Blackstone promised
he would never trust a
woman again, but sultry
Kelly Andrews was just
the woman to make him
break that vow! But was
it love or just lust that
irresistibly drew this
pair together?

*Available February 2004
at your favorite retail outlet.*

Silhouette Desire

Coming February 2004
from

SHERI WHITEFEATHER

Cherokee Stranger
(Silhouette Desire #1563)

James Dalton was the kind of man
a girl couldn't help but want.
The rugged stable manager exuded
sex, secrets...and danger. Local waitress
Emily Chapin had some secrets of her own.
The one thing neither could hide was
their burning need for each other!

*Available at your
favorite retail outlet.*

COMING NEXT MONTH

#1561 MAN BENEATH THE UNIFORM—Maureen Child
Dynasties: The Danforths
When Navy SEAL Zachary Sheriday was assigned to act as a
bodyguard to feisty Kimberly Danforth, he never considered he'd
be so drawn to his charge. Fiercely independent, and sexy, as well,
Kimberly soon had this buttoned-down military hunk completely
undone. But was this seduction one he was duty-bound to deny…?

#1562 THE MARRIAGE ULTIMATUM—Anne Marie Winston
Kristin Gordon had tried everything possible to get the attention of her
heart's desire: Dr. Derek Mahoney. But Derek's past haunted him, and
made him unwilling to act on the desire he felt for Kristin. Until one
steamy kiss set off a hunger that knew no bounds.

#1563 CHEROKEE STRANGER—Sheri WhiteFeather
He was everything a girl could want. James Dalton, rugged stable
manager, exuded sex…and danger. And for all her sweetness, local
waitress Emily Chapin had secrets of her own. One thing was
perilously clear: their burning need for each other!

#1564 BREATHLESS FOR THE BACHELOR—Cindy Gerard
Texas Cattleman's Club: The Stolen Baby
Sassy Carrie Whelan had always been a little in love with Ry Evans.
But as her big brother's best friend, Ry wasn't having it…until Carrie
decided to pursue another man. Suddenly the self-assured cowboy was
acting like a jealous lover and would do *anything* he could to make
Carrie his.

#1565 THE LONG HOT SUMMER—Rochelle Alers
The Blackstones of Virginia
Dormant desires flared the moment single dad Ryan Blackstone
laid eyes on Kelly Andrews. The sultry beauty was his son's teacher,
and Kelly's gentle manner was winning over both father and son. A
passionate affair with Kelly would be totally inappropriate…and
completely inescapable.

#1566 PLAYING BY THE BABY RULES—Michelle Celmer
Jake Carmichael considered himself a conscientious best friend. So
when Marisa Donato said she wanted a baby without the complications
of marriage, he volunteered to be the father. Their agreement was no
strings attached. But once pent-up passions ignited, those reasonable
rules were quickly thrown out the bedroom window!

SDCNM0104